DEFENDING ROXANNE

PJ FIALA

ROLLING THUNDER PUBLISHING

ALSO BY PJ FIALA

Click here to see a list of all of my books with the blurbs.

Contemporary Romance

Rolling Thunder Series

Moving to Love, Book 1

Moving to Hope, Book 2

Moving to Forever, Book 3

Moving to Desire, Book 4

Moving to You, Book 5

Moving Home, Book 6

Second Chances Series

Designing Samantha's Love, Book 1

Securing Kiera's Love, Book 2

Military Romantic Suspense

Bluegrass Security Series

Heart Thief, Book One

Finish Line, Book Two

Lethal Love, Book Three

The Bounty Hunters

Ford, Bounty Hunters Book One

Lincoln, Bounty Hunters Book Two

Dodge , Bounty Hunters Book Three

GHOST

GET TWO MORE EBOOKS - FREE!

Building a relationship with my readers is the very best thing about writing. I send monthly newsletters with details on new releases, special offers and other fun things relating to my books or prizes surrounding them.

If you sign up to my mailing list I'll send you all these books for free:

1. A copy of Moving to Love, Book 21 of the Rolling Thunder series.

2. A copy of Moving to Hope, Book 2 of the Rolling Thunder series.

3. A book list so you know what order to read my books in.

You can get the two novels **for free**, by signing up at https://www.subscribepage.com/PJsReadersClub

DEDICATION

I've had so many wonderful people come into my life and I want you all to know how much I appreciate it. From each and every reader who takes the time out of their day to read my stories and leave reviews, thank you.

My beautiful, smart and fun Road Queens, who play games with me, post fun memes, keep the conversation rolling and help me create these captivating characters, places, businesses and more. Thank you ladies for your ideas, support and love.

The following characters and places were created by:

Crowne Jewelers - Marilyn Oshnock Powell Marilyn should have been mentioned in Defending Sophie, and I apologize for my oversight.

Barb Keller named Hawk (Hank) Delany.

Kristi Hombs Kopydlowski gave Roxanne her last name - Bowman; and the Prime Minister's Assistant - Zacara Aliyeva.

Terri Merkel named Leland and Kay Bowman (Roxanne's parents), described Roxanne and named Raymond's father - Rowin Bowman.

Amy Higgison named Brendan Bowman.
Kerry Harteker named Matthew Bowman.
Bev Sten created Roxanne's history in that her father taught her how to use guns.
Ina-Ruth Berry Thies created the safe phrase "Everything is alright Luna".
Kelly Hungerford created Azerbaitani.
Shaina Fiala created the Prime Minister, Kanan Mommodov.
Denise Scott created Zacara's gamer name, Zaira.
Misty Whightsel created Raymond's gamer name - BackdoorScorcerer.
Lisa Murray named Leland's father, Darren Bowman.
Lisa Mettler named Carmela.
Cynthia Reifel named Hawk's best friend, Colt.
Lisa Flint Christianson named Hawk's wife, Sarah.
Nicky Ortiz picked the wedding songs.
Anita Shofner named the hotel, The Breeze Inn.
Sarah Brogni is my medical advisor.

A special thank you to Marijane Diodati, my amazing editor!

Last but not least, my family for the love and sacrifices they have made and continue to make to help me achieve this dream, especially my husband and best friend, Gene. Words can never express how much you mean to me, I Love You.

To our veterans and current serving members of our armed forces, police and fire departments, thank you ladies and gentlemen for your hard work and sacrifices;

it's with gratitude and thankfulness that I mention you in this dedication.

To Stacey!
Thank you for everything. "In it to win it!"

BLURB

Secrets and lies have become deadly.

While investigating the murder of her parents, Roxanne Bowman encounters more than she ever imagined she would. The secrets that both of her parents kept knock her off-kilter. Finding an intruder in their home in the process changes her life forever.

GHOST operative, Hawk Delany is back in the swing of things after being shot while on a mission. Sent to Washington, D.C. to investigate the murders of a foreign dignitary, and an American couple, the State Department Chief of Protocol and his wife, places him in a precarious position. The fight to help Roxanne solve the murders and to keep his heart from theft by the lovely Roxanne.

COPYRIGHT

Printed in the United States of America

First published 2019

Fiala, PJ

DEFENDING ROXANNE / PJ Fiala

p. cm.

I. Romance—Fiction.

2. Romance—Suspense.

3. Romance - Military

I. Title – DEFENDING ROXANNE

ISBN-13: 978-1-942618-89-8

"*Roxanne, it was weird, he looked like your dad's cousin, Raymond. Do you remember Raymond? He was always a bit different and he had so much trouble dealing with people. That's why when I saw this man following me, it completely scared the crap out of me. Then, I saw him again yesterday and I don't know what to do.*"

Roxanne's eyes flew open. Staring at the ceiling, her heart pounded in her chest as her mother's words came back to her. Throwing back the covers, she sat up and turned so her feet were touching the floor. Her childhood bedroom still had the same furniture, same bookcase across from her bed, same creeks in the floor. The only things that had changed were that her mother had repainted the room to a soft gray last year and had updated the bedding to match.

"I want you to be comfortable when you come home, and you've outgrown the pink floral patterns. This suits you so much better," her mother had said. Oh, how she wished she could speak to Mom now.

Sliding on her slipper socks, she walked out of her

room and hesitated. This home seemed too large and ominous somehow now. Glancing down the hall to her right, her parents' bedroom door was closed now and would be forever if it was up to her. But, only time would tell. Her brothers, Brendan and Matthew's, bedrooms were to her left. It had been her paternal grandparents' home before they passed, then her family's. Now it belonged to her and her brothers.

Descending the enormous, dark mahogany staircase with its white-painted handrails, which curved to the right of the large foyer in their old Georgetown home, she turned left and entered her parents' office.

Her mother had remodeled this room twenty years ago, but it still suited the era of the house. Majestic mahogany pillars stood adjacent to the wall behind her father's desk and in between those pillars were towering shelves of books. She loved playing in this room when she was a girl. Her father spent countless hours in here as his military career soared. His final position landed him at the State Department working as the Chief of Protocol, appointed by the President. It's also the position that got him and her mother killed.

Turning to the opposite side of the room, where her mother's identical desk sat, she walked behind the desk and opened the top left drawer. Somewhere in here her mother had kept the key to the storage units in the basement. She needed to find a picture of Raymond. Her first order of business tomorrow morning would be to find Raymond and figure out why he had been stalking her mother and if he had anything to do with her death. The sheer level of chaos, not to mention the political uproar, that had enveloped her parents' deaths and that of Kanan Mammodov, Prime Minister of Azerbaitani at the same time was monumental. Feeling around the papers in the drawer, she also found office supplies, staples, tape, and a ruler but she couldn't feel the key. The moonlight that shone through the tall windows to her right was ample light for moving around the house, but didn't offer enough light to see a small key. Yet, she enjoyed this darkness and the anonymity it offered. There had been at a minimum a handful of reporters on the street in front of the house since her parents died two weeks ago. Turning on the lights would allow them to see in better and use the zoom lenses on their cameras. Fuck that.

Pulling the papers out of the drawer and laying them on top of the clean desk, she felt around a bit more. Nothing.

The top drawer on the right was next. Pulling the multitude of tablets and notepads from the drawer, she felt around the bottom of the drawer and found nothing. Repeating this motion for the five remaining drawers on each side, she had a mess to show for her efforts laying all around her and still no key. Standing with her hands on her hips, she looked across the room to her father's desk, then remembered, he'd hidden things on the underside of drawers from time to time. Pulling out the top right drawer of her mother's desk, she ran her hands underneath and smiled when she felt an envelope taped to the underside. Peeling the tape away and pulling the envelope from underneath, she smiled to herself as she removed the key and stepped over her mess to make her way to the basement. Through the foyer and into the living room, she turned right and headed to the back of the house and the kitchen.

The basement door was directly to the right of the entrance to the kitchen. Opening the door, she clicked on the light and descended to the basement. Over the years her parents had reinforced the basement and added lighting and the locked storage units, which her father had insisted upon having, since his position meant he had access to and possession of confidential information. Her mother then had insisted they have a room in the basement where family heirlooms and pictures were stored, keeping the room at a constant temperature and humidity free.

Opening her mom's storage room, she looked at the shelves, walking down the row until she found the storage boxes marked "Family Photos." Her mother, ever the organizer, had them stored by year. Trying to recall the last time they'd seen Raymond, she remembered being around ten, which was twenty-nine years ago. Finding this box and pulling it down from the shelf with both hands, she turned to take it upstairs and lay the photographs out on the dining room table.

At the top of the steps, she nudged the light switch with her right elbow and closed the door with her behind. Turning to her left, she headed into the dining room from the kitchen and set the box on top of the table.

A noise from her parents' office caused her to freeze. Papers softly shuffling, then nothing. Slowly reaching around her back, her heartbeat increased rapidly, and dread filled her gut as she realized she'd left her gun upstairs in her nightstand. Shit.

Softly she crept to the door of the dining room which was directly behind the huge staircase she'd come down earlier. Staying close to the wall she listened again. Inhaling, she took a slow deep breath and crept out of the room and around the staircase.

A massive hulk emerged from the office, and she froze

for only a moment before turning to run in the opposite direction. The backdoor was in the kitchen; if she could get there, she'd run across the lawn and to the neighbor's home for help.

Three steps from the kitchen she was grabbed from behind, an iron band of arm around her waist and one hand over her mouth. She was pulled into the hardened chest of her attacker and barely able to move. Her left arm was trapped next to her body in the steel grip of the man who now began to drag her deeper into her home.

Panic flooded her brain and her stomach. She struggled to get free, twisting her body as much as she could, hoping to find a weakness to exploit. She began kicking back, but her slipper socks weren't going to do any damage to this man. A second man appeared in her peripheral vision and chuckled, before saying, "Well, Hawk, looks like you found yourself a thief."

2

"Jesus, stop kicking me, you little thief." He carried her effortlessly, almost, but she was squirming and thrashing around. She was thin, but tall for a woman. He'd guess her to be 5'9" or so. "Wyatt, pull that chair out for me."

Wyatt chuckled. He was enjoying this far too much, but he did pull a dining room chair away from the table so Hawk could deposit his wriggling parcel. Plopping her down without a lot of grace, he held his hand firmly on her shoulder. "If you try to run, I'll tase you and trust me, you won't like that. Understand?"

The moonlight streamed through the large windows and he could see the angry glint in her eyes. The bluish glow from the moon reflected in them, made him feel she could be other-worldly. She didn't say a word to him, so he squeezed her shoulder hard enough to get a response from her.

"Ouch, asshole."

"You didn't answer."

"Yes. You'll tase me if I run. Got it. Now get your fucking hand off of me."

Wyatt laughed so hard he even slapped his knee. "For chrissakes, Hawk, she's got a hell of a temper on her."

"Well, she'd better get over her temper, she's been caught breaking and entering."

"What?" His captive yelled. "I'm not the one breaking and entering, you dolt. You two are. I live here. This is my home you fucking idiots."

Wyatt laughed again, "I'd love to get this recorded. Aren't you the least bit worried about this situation?

"If I were you two, I'd be afraid. First of all, there are reporters everywhere outside all the flipping time including right now, watching my house. Second, I doubt you know who I am, but once you find out, you'll be shaking in your giant boots."

"Wyatt, we're going to be shaking in our boots. I haven't shaken in my boots in..." He rubbed his jaw, clearly enjoying his little cat and mouse game. "Aw, shit, I've never shaken in my boots."

"Classy." She spat out and he grinned. Her anger was kind of funny. She turned her eyes back to him and in a calmer voice said, "Look at me. I'm wearing yoga pants, a tank top and slipper socks. Do you honestly think I'd break into a house with slipper socks on?"

"Could be a ruse."

Even though the light was dim, he saw her roll her eyes. "Oh, for chrissakes. Just my luck to get broken into by a couple of dumb giants."

She started to stand but he placed his hand firmly on her left shoulder and pushed her back into the chair. "Move again, and I'll tie you up."

"Sorry, I'm not really into BDSM."

"Then you surely won't like being tied to a dining room chair while we finish our investigation."

"Investigation? Do you really call breaking and entering an investigation?"

He looked at Wyatt who was grinning like a fool.

Glancing at a box on the dining room table, Hawk asked, "What were you looking for in this box?"

He lifted the lid on the box. It was filled with photo albums.

Pulling the first photo album from the box, Hawk began looking at the pictures as well as he could with the only lighting from the moonlight streaming in through the tall narrow windows. The Bowman family around thirty years ago it seemed. Their children were now in their 40's, except the daughter who was reportedly 39, were around the ages of 10 to 14 in these pictures. Their daughter, Roxanne, with her white-blond hair stood in front of her mother, Kay, with her similar coloring. The two sons, Brendan and Matthew, stood on either side of her, their hair darker blond but they had similar coloring. The father, Leland, with his sandy-brown, short-cropped hair and perfect posture, stood next to Kay, all of them smiling except little Roxanne. It looked to be around Easter, as the females were wearing pink dresses that spoke of springtime and Easter Sunday. Studying the background of the picture, it was the front of this house. This had been a family home for years.

Looking again at the little girl in the pictures, his eyes slowly looked up and landed on the woman sitting in the chair before him. Same look of displeasure on her face. Same nose. Same hair color.

Looking at Kay Bowman's picture, he saw the resemblance immediately. "If you're Roxanne Bowman what are you doing rummaging through your parents' office, leaving a mess behind and digging boxes of pictures out? And, all of this in the dark I might add."

"Well, I'd ask you why you're lurking around in the dark in a home that doesn't belong to you in the middle of the night and all dressed in black. You have weapons all over your body, but you want me to believe you aren't here to rob me or cause me harm."

"I asked you first." He was beginning to waiver on his belief that this woman before him was a thief and it had nothing to do with the fact that she was clearly a beauty.

She crossed her arms over her ample chest, which he was silently happy about because her nipples poked out of that skimpy tank top she wore, and it was beginning to make his eyes wander.

He continued. "Okay, I'll give a little, then you give a little." She tossed her head slightly and he took that as agreement. "My colleague and I are here looking for clues as to the Bowman's murders. Your turn."

"Clues like what?"

"Like who killed them and why?"

"Why do you think you'll find those clues here?"

"I don't know if we'll find anything. But it seemed like a good place to start." He squatted in front of her to look her in the eye. "What are you doing lurking around in the dark?"

She took in a deep breath, hesitated as if trying to decide if she'd answer or not, then finally said, "I didn't turn the lights on because there are always reporters skulking, sneaking around outside. Some of the windows, like those in the office, don't have blinds that I can close."

"We didn't see any reporters out there."

"Sometimes, they're blatant. Sometimes, they hide.

Even in plain sight. I'll bet if there was someone out there, and they saw you breaking in, it's already on Twitter."

Glancing at Wyatt, he saw his comrade pull his phone from his pocket and tap on it a few times. Wyatt shook his head slowly. "What goes bump in the night? The President is up to something. Masked men in the Bowman house."

Closing her eyes, the blond before him sighed. "They'll be out in droves before long. Again."

The rapid beating of her heart began to slow as she began thinking these men weren't here to do her harm. But the jury was still out. They weren't beating her, tying her up or trying to hurt her in any other way. Yet. And the fact that they were attempting to have a discussion with her made her hopeful.

The big, dark man with the mesmerizing green eyes, squatting in front of her took in a deep breath. "Tell me why you were scowling in this picture."

He turned the photo album in his hand so she could see the picture. It was Easter Sunday 29 years ago. Her family had just come back from church and she wanted to search for Easter eggs. She'd beat her brothers the past two years with the amount of eggs she'd found. Her Grandfather Bowman secretly gave each of his grandchildren a penny for every egg they found. The winner earned an additional twenty-five cents. She wanted to win.

"I wanted to hunt for eggs, but my mom wouldn't stop taking an insane number of pictures. She had photographers here to chronicle our entire day. We'd just sat through a ridiculously long church sermon. Had to endure countless church ladies pinching our cheeks and admiring our Easter clothes and then the long and boring receiving line for my father because he'd just been promoted again."

His eyes never left her face, she could tell he was studying her. Looking for a clue that she was lying. It was difficult to tell in this lighting, but it appeared his eyes glinted. The other man, it was hard to see him, he was in her peripheral vision.

He chuckled. His voice was deep and rich when he spoke again. "Did you win?"

"Damn straight I did."

"So, what are you looking for in these photo albums at..." Glancing at his watch he finished. "Two in the morning in the dark?"

"Why don't you tell me first who the hell you are and what you're doing in my house?"

The second man laughed again and walked to stand in front of her. His hands were at his sides, almost as if he was ready to pull a gun to use on her. His hair was dark, not as dark as the man before her, but his eyes were light, they looked almost amber, maybe a bit cat-like and it set her nerves on edge. He had a scar that ran down his left cheek, curved down the back of his neck and disappeared into his t-shirt and it set her nerves on edge. What on earth had happened to him to get that scar? He continued to stare, saying nothing, but he was on alert.

The man crouching before her finally stood. He held his right hand out to her, "My name's Hawk." Tilting his head to the right to indicate his partner, he finished. "This is my colleague, Wyatt. We were sent here to help investigate the murders of your parents and Prime Minister Kanan Mammodov."

She looked at his hand, still held out for her to take. She had to stifle a nervous giggle as the thought ran through her mind that it could be described as a bear paw due to its size. Straightening her spine, she reached out and placed her hand in his. His fingers wrapped around her hand making her feel small and delicate which didn't happen often. She was tall for a woman at 5'9" without heels on. This meant she often towered over her female counterparts at work and a few of the men, a fact that she often used to her advantage when dealing with some of the more difficult personalities in her office.

Adding pressure to convey that she was not afraid of him, though she wasn't completely convinced of his friendliness yet, she saw the corners of his mouth turn up slightly.

"Who sent you here?"

Continuing to hold her hand, his rich smooth voice answered, "I'm not at liberty to say."

Quickly pulling her hand away, partly because now she was pissed again and partly because she liked the way her hand felt in his, she snapped, "Really? And I'm just supposed to believe you."

"If you hadn't been here, which you weren't supposed to be, you'd never have known we were. And, it would seem, at least on the surface, that we're on the same side. Don't you want to know who murdered your parents and the Prime Minister?"

"Of course, I do. But, I don't like being in the dark."

Both men laughed at her comment, since, clearly, here they sat in the dark. "You know what I mean."

Wyatt finally said, "We don't even know you, how would we know what you mean?"

"Right, well, why don't you let me go upstairs and get my purse so I can show you my ID."

Hawk's jaw tightened. "You have a weapon upstairs?"

"No."

"I don't believe you. The intelligence we have says that Roxanne Bowman has a concealed carry permit, trains regularly and is a pretty good shot. It's unlikely you wouldn't have a firearm upstairs."

Her nose twitched in displeasure as he clearly knew things about her that would be in a dossier due to her father's security clearances and the family's constant background checks.

Tossing her head back, she looked Hawk in the eyes. He didn't back down. Normally she could stare men and women down and they'd look away first. Not this guy. "Fine. I have a firearm upstairs."

"How many?"

"One."

"Where is it?"

Taking a deep breath, she thought about how to answer. Then figuring they'd just ransack the place if they wanted, she said, "It's in my nightstand."

Wyatt disappeared and she assumed he was headed upstairs to go through her nightstand. They'd better not steal her gun; it was the one her father had given her for her birthday when she turned 35.

Turning another chair away from the table and sliding it in front of her, Hawk sat and faced her. He didn't sit back in a relaxed position, but he didn't look stiff and uncomfortable.

"Why are you here on a Thursday night, don't you have to work tomorrow?"

Swallowing, she stared into his eyes. She liked that he didn't waiver or cower. It was refreshing and different. "My boss gave me a couple more weeks off to try and work through my parent's deaths. I'm so puzzled why the Bureau of Diplomatic Security, FBI or police can't find out who killed them. I know it's only been a couple of weeks. But the President is beginning to take a lot of heat for it because, of course, the government of Azerbaitani wants answers."

"What are you going to do to help solve their murders?"

"I don't know. But, I've tried talking to local police, the FBI, and the State Department and they don't want to hear anything I have to say. I don't have any evidence, my brothers and I have given statements and their investigation leads them elsewhere. I'd hoped I could find something that would make them see that I had information."

"What information do you have, Roxanne?"

4

He watched her face for signs of lying. She was good if she was lying, no detectible eye shifting to the left and up, no subtle hand movements indicating nervousness on her account. Her voice didn't shake, and he got the distinct impression that she was good, very good under pressure. Then again, their intelligence said she was an attorney, so she'd no doubt be embroiled in sticky situations on a daily basis.

"I still don't know who you are other than Hawk. Who sent you here to delve through my home and belongings, are you friend or foe?"

Wyatt walked into the room with two guns, which he lay on the dining room table, at the far end. And her purse. He promptly dug through her purse and pulled out her wallet. Taking his time, he unsnapped the clasp and flipped it open. Turning slightly so the moonlight would aid his reading, he was silent for a minute more.

His eyes then snapped up and caught his. "Roxanne Bowman. Age 39, Lives in Chestertown, Maryland."

Looking back at Roxanne he said quietly, "You said you had one gun."

Her lips twitched slightly, but she didn't allow herself to smile.

Hawk stood and heaved out a breath. "So, we can play this two ways as I see it. You can start being honest with us or we can tie you up and leave you here until someone comes to find you. I'll probably call the press or a maid." He looked around the massive room with its old Georgetown presence and charm, but clearly too large for a woman who worked 90 minutes away to maintain, so there was likely staff.

"I've said this before; I still don't know who you are."

"Okay." Pushing the chair away he'd recently sat in, he crouched down before her again. Mostly because his side was cramping up today. He'd never had the issue before, but after having been shot a couple months ago, he experienced these damned muscle cramps.

"What if I said, 'everything is alright, Luna?'"

He watched her eyes as the dawning came over her. They crackled first with surprise, then with a softness that belied her tough exterior. Her spine stiffened. Her mouth began to open, but she promptly closed it. He knew those words, her family's secret code words for her, would surprise her.

"How did you know to say that?"

He stood and stepped away from her, crossing his arms over his chest. Choosing not to respond to her he waited her out.

She stood then and a couple of things hit him. She was tall for a woman, but still looked small to him. Her hair was long but braided in the back and he wanted to see what it looked like flowing over her shoulders, which were clearly defined in the moonlight, the skimpy tank top she wore showed them off perfectly. She slammed her hands on her hips when he remained silent and her breasts jiggled with the movement, which, dammit, he was unable to resist sneaking a look at.

"Eyes up here, buddy." She sternly half-yelled pointing to her eyes.

He chuckled and she was right, he shouldn't have looked. But, fuck, her breasts were a sight.

"Who. Told. You. Our. Code?"

Taking a deep breath, he replied, "The person who hired us told us the code in case we had trouble with any family members. I know the codes for all of you."

"My brothers just suck. They should have told me what they were up to." She took a few steps to the left, turned and paced back to her spot in front of the chair. Turning she repeated her previous steps, muttering to herself and dammit, he felt sorry for her brothers when she saw them next. The words 'cut their nuts off' came out twice along with 'a stern ass kicking', which in his mind was so much better than having their nuts cut off. If they got the choice.

Stopping in front of him, he clamped his jaw together and forced his eyes to stare at hers and not her fine breasts, not to mention her nipples were poking out of that tank top like she was standing in below zero weather. He was going to need to get laid soon after witnessing this beauty.

"Why Luna?" He asked it before he thought about what he was going to say.

"None of your business."

"I can guess."

"I don't care. Which one of my soon-to-be-nutless brothers hired you?"

He held his hands up to ward off her words. "I didn't say either of them did. I simply said the person who hired us."

"They are the only ones who..." She froze and locked eyes with him. His heart began racing at the look in hers. Icy blue irises looked ethereal in the moonlight and so full of expression. He'd bet she couldn't play poker to save her life. Maybe he'd play some strip poker with her and get her naked so he could see...

"My dad's best friend, Wade is the only other person who knew our codes in case of an emergency."

Her eyes narrowed as she watched his face for any expression. Luckily, he had years of training in such circumstances with much more ruthless opponents.

"Look, I'll save you a ton of shit here, I don't know the identity of the person who hired us. I didn't take the call, I didn't talk to him, my colleague did."

"Who, Wyatt here?"

Wyatt chuckled, but was busy looking through the photo albums. "Why don't you tell us what you're looking for in these pictures? We can find it or him or her and be on our way. Or maybe you like talking to us."

Her jaw tightened as she scowled at Wyatt, who never looked up from the photo album in his hand. Turning it so he could see, Wyatt teased, "Look Hawk, little Roxanne had short bangs in this picture and a dolly."

Roxanne lunged across the table to take the photo album away, but Wyatt danced out of the way, chuckling. "I won't say anything more if you just tell us what you were looking for."

He felt sorry for her and Wyatt could be a handful when he wanted to be. Right now, he was getting sick of Roxanne's silence and it was showing. "Roxanne." She turned to face him, her back ramrod straight, irritation written all over her face. "We're friendly. Our contact wouldn't have given us your codes if he thought there was any danger in us having them. We were asked by our contact to help solve the murders of your parents and the Prime Minister."

She heaved out a breath, crossed her arms over her ample chest, thank fuck, and after a few moments of silence, said, "My mom told me about a week before she was killed that she saw my dad's cousin, Raymond following her. Raymond was a little off-center or not quite right in the head. Something to do with a high fever as a child or whatever. Anyway, we haven't seen Raymond in close to thirty years, so I wanted to remind myself what he looked like."

"Then you were going to find him and ask him why he was following your mom?"

The slight shrug of her right shoulder was all he got in response. "If he's not right in the head, that's not very smart."

She sucked in a deep breath, held it for a second then let it out slowly. "For all I know he wanted to make contact again."

"Then why wouldn't he have said something to her?"

She rubbed her temples with the fingers of both hands before saying anything. "You're asking me to guess what someone with a mental disorder is going to do or what his intentions are. I have no idea. I just thought if I saw him face-to-face, I'd be able to tell if he was lying."

"What if he meant to do her harm?"

5

None of this made any sense. All she knew is that she heard her mother's voice in her sleep and took it as a sign that her mom was trying to help her figure this out.

"So, let's do this." Hawk pointed to the box she'd carried upstairs filled with photo albums. "Let's spread these out on the table and look through them. Wyatt and I won't be able to help much, other than see if someone is in a picture that we don't recognize from our intel. But, that seems to be as good a place to start as any."

She responded, "We don't have window shades in this room, just the sheers, so turning on the lights will give the reporters outside a chance to see in."

Hawk shrugged one of his bulky shoulders but Wyatt said, "Let's throw some sheets over the windows."

That would work for what they needed to do. "Better yet, we have a linen closet in the kitchen with all of our tablecloths. I'll go and grab those." She started walking to the kitchen and Hawk followed her. "You think I'm going to run?"

"I have no idea what you're going to do, so let's just say I'm being cautiously optimistic that we're working together."

"Suit yourself." She walked through the kitchen to the pantry just off to the right and pulled open the linen closet door. Grabbing six tablecloths she turned and handed them to Hawk, then turned and grabbed a couple more. When he waited for her, she wrinkled her nose a bit but proceeded him into the dining room.

Hawk and Wyatt began slinging the tablecloths over the windows and she couldn't help herself from looking at them. Well, Hawk actually. The man was massive. Around 6'8", he was built and solid. Tall enough to tuck the table-cloths behind the curtain rods without so much as standing on his toes. Still, no matter how impressive he was, she needed to get out of here. First, she'd call her brothers and make sure they didn't hire Hawk and company, then she'd call Wade. The need to know what was going on was overriding everything else right now.

She began pulling photo albums from the box, lining them up along the long dining room table. As she approached the end where her guns lay, Wyatt turned and locked eyes with her. His were cat-like. Amber in color they held an exotic hint to them. He wore a long-sleeved shirt but it defined the muscles beneath. A chill ran through her at the way he looked at her, it was almost as if he'd be just fine if she fell over dead; he'd step over her and keep on going.

"What's going on?" Hawk turned to see them staring at each other.

Wyatt answered before she could. "She was inching toward the guns here."

"I was laying out the photo albums so we could go through them."

"MmHm." He harrumped and she clamped her jaw together to keep from saying something she might regret. When he picked her guns up and slid them easily in the back waistband of his tactical pants, she narrowed her eyes at him.

"You'd better not steal my guns. One of them was a birthday gift from my father. I will call the police."

"Look, Princess, I don't need your fucking guns. But since we know you're a liar and can't be trusted I'm sure as fuck not going to let you have them."

"Listen here you son of a..."

"That's enough." Hawk's voice boomed. She stopped staring at Wyatt and turned her attention to Hawk. Angry Hawk was scary. His black hair, a bit longer on top than the sides and back, gleamed in the moonlight, his light eyes were in such contrast to the rest of him that she felt transfixed totally unable to look away. "He won't steal your guns. But, he has a point. We don't know that we can trust each other yet."

He looked at Wyatt and barked, "Stop needling her, we have shit to do here."

"You're down-right chatty tonight, Hawk. Anything to do with the company?" Wyatt sneered before going back to covering the windows and she went back to laying out the photo albums. Hawk picked up the empty box and dropped it on the floor across the room. Wyatt finished with the last window and walked to the light switch on the wall and turned on the lights. She heard him whistle long and low and looked over at him to see him looking around the room.

Glancing then at Hawk, she saw he was looking at her.

She felt the flush run up her torso all the way to her hair, her nipples pebbled and goose bumps rose on her skin. Swallowing the lump in her throat, she looked away from the intensity in his eyes and began looking through the photo albums. Relief swept through her when Hawk and Wyatt did the same. Flipping through page after page she had to work hard not to sit and wax nostalgic at her family in happier days. Finally, Hawk said, "This looks like a family reunion or something."

Leaning over the table to see what he was looking at, she saw the annual picnic pictures with her dad's side of the family. "Yes, our annual Bowman Bonanza."

Wyatt laughed. "Somehow Bonanza doesn't go with this place."

"That was the point. Grandma Bowman wanted us to shed our public personas for a couple of hours and have fun in a different way. So, the Bonanza was just that. Ring toss, horseshoes, hula hoops, one year we had a clown."

She glanced at the four pictures on the page but didn't see Raymond. Standing to walk around the table so she wasn't looking at the book upside down Hawk slid it toward her when she neared him.

She turned the page and there he was, sitting in a lawn chair, a drink in his hand, a vacant look in his eyes. "That's him." He was a nice looking man with his blond hair and green eyes. He was clean shaven and wearing some wild colored sweatpants and a blue t-shirt.

Hawk leaned in and his shoulder brushed her arm. Her tummy felt like butterflies were flitting around inside but she didn't pull away. "Did he always have that vacant stare?"

"Yes. But it was deceiving. You didn't think he was paying attention, but he heard and saw everything."

"Then why did you say he wasn't right in the head?"

She looked over at Hawk, and his piercing green eyes were looking at hers. He hadn't shaven in a couple of days and the black scruff of beard added to the mystery of him and made the lightness of his eyes more pronounced. "He said he heard voices and sometimes he would just start talking as if he was having a conversation with someone who wasn't there. He'd speak full sentences and wait while the invisible person said something back to him."

"Did he ever lose consciousness?"

"I don't know, Hawk. I was ten the last time I saw him. I just thought he was weird and I stayed away from him. But my mom would sit and talk to him sometimes. She said she felt sorry for him because the rest of the family just tolerated him or kept their distance. She thought he must be awfully lonely. Dad would say he had all his imaginary friends to keep him company."

She turned the page to scour the photographs for more pictures of Raymond. He was in a couple of them. Then she saw a picture of her mom sitting in a lawn chair in front of Raymond talking to him. She had a slight smile on her face and Raymond did too, like they just shared a secret. It hurt her heart a little bit to see her mom with Raymond. Especially if he was the one who killed her.

Clearing her throat, she said, "Do you guys want some coffee or tea?"

Hawk replied first, "No, thank you, but go ahead if you want some."

Wyatt echoed his comrade. Hawk reached for another photo album and she slipped the picture of her mom and Raymond from the photo album in front of her turning the page so the picture wouldn't be missed. Walking into the kitchen, she tucked the picture into the waistband of her yoga pants and pulled a coffee cup from the cupboard and set it on the Keurig Machine. Selecting the coffee flavor she wanted, she set it inside the machine and pushed the power button to warm it up. Glancing out the window she saw dawn was beginning to break, she had maybe another forty-five minutes of darkness before the sun would come up. The machine beeped that it had warmed, and she pushed the button to begin brewing her cup. The noise of the machine gave her enough cover to slip across the floor quietly and to the basement stairs.

6

The whirring of the Keurig machine was almost hypnotic. He'd been awake for twenty hours now and the warmth of the house and the aroma of freshly brewed coffee plus the white noise of the machine threatened to lull him to sleep.

Quickly standing, he stretched then headed to the kitchen to wake himself up. What he saw, or more accurately, didn't see, woke him up quickly. "Shit."

Taking long strides, he walked to the corner of the room where the linen closet was to see if there was another door. Seeing nothing, he walked to the backdoor to see it locked. Turning his body in the opposite direction he saw a door slightly ajar. Three steps and he was across the floor, whipping it open he saw it went to the basement. "Wyatt, she's on the run."

Thundering down the steps he found the flashlight on his belt and unclipped the carabiner at the same time as he hit the button on the end to turn it on. Flashing it across the walls he found a light switch and immediately flipped it on, illuminating the basement. There were doors everywhere. He began opening doors to see if she was down here and found a bathroom, a cellar room with stores of canned foods. One room held what looked like Christmas decorations. He found the storage room with the photo albums. Another room was locked and finally across the main room was the last door he had yet to check. Whipping it open he found a long dark tunnel.

"Fuck. Fuck. Fuck."

Using his flashlight once more he looked for a light and found one easily. A trail of clothing greeted his eyes next. Roxanne's yoga pants lay on the floor. A couple of steps after was the white tank top she'd worn and then her slipper socks. There was a long board with 5 hooks on the right side of the tunnel and 3 of those hooks held backpacks.

"What do we have?" Wyatt asked as he caught up to him.

"We have two missing backpacks and one missing woman."

"Slippery little witch." Wyatt pulled his phone from his pocket and tapped it a few times. Hawk began unzipping the other backpacks to see what was inside. Clothing, shoes, money, and a gun, 9mm and an extra loaded magazine in each one.

Not good. She had clothes, money and a weapon.

Behind him Wyatt spoke into his phone. "Roxanne Bowman is on the run. She was here when we got here and now she's in the wind. She has money, clothing and a weapon, which looks to be a 9mm handgun."

Hawk began following the tunnel to the other end and found one of the missing backpacks laying on the floor, unzipped with clothing spilling from it. Picking it up he saw no money and no weapon, no clip, she had two guns and ammo.

Continuing on, he followed the tunnel, which appeared to be similar to a concrete culvert inserted into the ground. It was dry, which meant it was sealed, though it smelled musty, which made sense. A noise above him caused him to run, where he found three steps fashioned from rebar and inserted into the side. On the top rung was a foot, connected to Roxanne, he assumed. Reaching up he was able to grab her ankle and hold on while trying not to fall off the small steps.

Concerned he'd hurt her he tried being gentle, but he couldn't let her get away. Tugging as gently as he could, he heard her swearing. In order to kick him with her other foot, she'd have to drop it through the hole which would likely send her falling to the ground below. She tried valiantly to kick him away, shake him off, anything to get rid of him, but he was hanging on tight.

Wyatt finally made it to him. Climbing on one side of the minuscule step he reached up and grabbed her leg closer to her knee.

"You fuckers. God dammit let me go." She twisted her body so she was in a sitting position and put her other foot through the hole in order to kick at Wyatt. She landed a good blow on his forearm which made a string of curse words spew from his mouth and possibly a threat if she did it again.

She tried kicking once more and this time he was ready. He could see her rear her foot back..."You got this, Wyatt?" he asked softly.

"Yeah." He huffed. He was beginning to tire, but so was Roxanne; he could tell she wasn't pulling as hard as she had previously.

Just as her other foot came down through the hole, he let go of her ankle and grabbed her second foot.

"You son-of-a-bitch." She swore. But, defeat settled and she stopped trying to fight. Maybe it was the realization that if they pulled her through the hole, she'd likely fall to the ground.

He began pulling her down through the hole and she yelled, "Wait, I'll fall, wait..."

But, just like peeling off a band aid, he quickly pulled her down, and both he and Wyatt grabbed a body part. He let go of her leg and grabbed her around the waist, firmly pulling her against his body; Wyatt wrestled with her arms, which were raised in a position to hit them.

"Don't do it, Roxanne. I'm not in the fucking mood." Wyatt warned and it must have been the tone of his voice, 'cause he felt the breath leave her lungs and her arms settled on his shoulders to steady herself.

Stepping down the bottom step, he half jostled her, half tossed her up in the air to position her better against him, and actually threw her over his shoulder to carry her out of the tunnel. They'd have to find a way to lock that door so she couldn't pull this little stunt again.

"Put me down, I'll walk." She pleaded, but he had no intention of letting her run again. She was costing them time and money right now.

Wyatt's phone chipped behind him as they neared the basement area of the house. "Jax, Dodge and Axel are on their way."

"Did you tell them we found her?"

"Yeah, they're still coming 'cause apparently we now need someone to babysit."

"Jax say that?"

"Yep."

He chuckled. Jax was their first female operative in GHOST and one badass chick. She was the toughest in her unit in the Army and had sharpshooter status, she could sass talk with the best of them, and she was seldom afraid of anything when they were on missions.

"Jax will straighten you out, Roxanne. It'll be fun to watch."

7

She was so pissed right now. At herself more than anything. She shouldn't have shed her clothes, that's what slowed her up. But, she honestly thought if they didn't know what she was wearing, it would be harder for them to find her. Dammit.

Being carried like a cave woman was pissing her off just a little bit more. It was also hard on her ribs and made it difficult to breathe.

Finally Hawk turned to ascend the basement steps. She'd soon be out of this position, but she wasn't sure if that was a good thing or not. And, there was maybe a bit of trepidation about this Jax person. Hopefully she was short, that would be an advantage she could exploit.

At the top of the steps, Hawk bent over and set her on her feet. That's when he looked at her. Their eyes locked for a moment, then his eyes traveled down her body. At first it almost felt like a sensual caress, then his lips turned up into a grin. Wyatt came up behind Hawk, stopped, stared at her, looked her up and down and burst out laughing.

"What the fuck kind of clothing are you wearing? I mean, the 90's called and they want their clothing back."

"Shut up."

That just made him laugh all the harder, she could still hear him laughing as he walked into the dining room. Hawk stood perfectly still, but he still had that damned grin on his face.

"Go ahead and say it, I know you want to, then this conversation can be over." She had on her favorite t-shirt from around twenty years ago, a deep red Tee that was barely long enough to cover her breasts, which were larger than they were when this was her favorite Tee, with bright pink fringes that hung close to her navel. The low-slung denim jeans she wore lay on her hips and left a large expanse of bare mid-drift exposed. Her tennis shoes were the only things that fit decently and no one was looking at them.

He just shook his head, held his arm out to the side and motioned to the dining room, "Let's go, Luna, we've got some work to do."

"Don't call me that."

"Why not, it's a nickname isn't it?"

Pressing her lips together she stalked to the dining room and plopped down in the chair she'd sat in previously.

"You didn't answer."

"Because I didn't want to."

Hawk chuckled.

"Seriously, don't you know you're supposed to check your go bag often to make sure everything in it is still okay and...fits."

"Stop. Yes, I know. My dad had been bugging me recently to do just that, but I've been busy."

"Did he always bug you to check your go bag?"

"No. Just the past couple of months he'd been nagging."

She saw the look Hawk sent Wyatt's way, and Wyatt stopped digging through the photo albums and stared at her.

Hawk pulled a chair away from the table and spun it to face her. Sitting, he leaned his forearms on his thighs and locked eyes with her. "Why do you think your father recently was more insistent that you check your go bag?"

"I don't kn..." She froze. Why would her dad start bugging her about her go bag? She stared into Hawk's green eyes; it was difficult not to. They were simply beautiful if you could call a man's eyes beautiful. Something about the light shade of green against his olive skin and black hair. But also, he looked like a man that just overturned a clue.

"Was he also asking your brothers to check their go bags?"

"I don't know, I could ask. But neither of my brothers live close. One is in Japan with his family. He's the Ambassador for the United States to Japan. My other brother lives in South Carolina. He's still in the service and is stationed at Camp LeJeune. Since neither of them get back here very often, I can't see why he'd bother."

"Was there anything else he had asked you that you thought was unusual?" Hawk leaned back in his chair and crossed his arms over his massive chest.

She took a deep breath and watched him study her face. Her heart beat a bit faster and she suddenly felt flushed even though she was largely exposed and wouldn't mind a sweater. "He asked me a question that I thought was strange a couple of weeks before he was murdered. He asked me if I'd noticed anything unusual lately." She fidgeted with her fingers in the fringes and tried recalling that conversation with her dad.

"He'd called me and asked me if I'd noticed anything out of sorts." Crossing her arms in front of her, more to warm herself than anything she waited for Hawk or Wyatt to respond.

Wyatt walked over to stand next to Hawk, then he squatted down and asked, "Did you ask him what he meant by that or what he thought you should notice?"

"I asked him to give me specifics and he just responded that I always had to watch out for myself because a single woman alone was a target or something like that."

"And you didn't find that alarming?"

She shook her head, "Not really. He always taught me to be self-sufficient. He was the one who trained me to shoot guns. He made sure I received self-defense lessons. He always made sure I was able to take care of myself."

Hawk leaned forward again. "Did your father know that his cousin Raymond was following your mom? Or someone who looked like Raymond?"

"No. Mom said she didn't want to bother him with this because he had been preoccupied recently with Prime Minister Mammodov's visit. She said he'd spent more time on the phone than ever before and she didn't know why this particular visit was getting so much more of his attention than any other dignitary's visit."

Hawk stood and gently pushed the chair back under the table where he'd gotten it from. Wyatt stood at the same time. When Hawk turned around, he said to Wyatt, "Snap some pictures of Raymond and send them to Jax, Dodge and Axel. Then send them to Gaige and ask him to locate Raymond. Once we have an address, we'll go pay him a visit."

Oh, no way was she missing this. "I'm going with you."

"No, you aren't, Roxanne."

She stood so fast she almost tipped the chair over. "I am too going and nothing you can say will stop me. I'm the person who told you about him and he just may be the person who killed my parents. I want to look him in the eye and ask him if he killed my parents."

"Then what, Roxanne? You think he'll just crumble and say, 'Oh you got me.'." Hawk mocked.

"I'm sure he won't but I still want to see the recognition on his face. See how he responds."

"Look, I agree that you probably have more of a right than anyone to speak to Raymond about your parents, especially your mom, but we're on a mission and we can't bring a civilian in like this."

He glanced at Wyatt who simply grinned and nodded.

Hawk replied. "Wyatt."

That got Wyatt walking to the end of the table and begin snapping pictures. She didn't understand what that meant, but then again, she didn't want to. But, she was going to speak with Raymond, no matter what she had to do to get there.

8

H is phone chirped signaling a text. Pulling it from his pocket, he looked up at Wyatt. "The rest of the team is here."

Wyatt chuckled, "You're about to meet Jax."

"Big deal." Wyatt laughed as he turned and headed to the front door.

"They're just going to walk in the front door with the press outside?"

"That's how we came in."

"And the press saw you. And, how did you know the passcode to get into the house."

He simply stared at her. He watched her process his stare and the second it dawned that the person who hired them also gave them the code for entry into the house, he saw her jaw tighten and cute little nose wrinkle.

"Are there any secrets he didn't tell you?"

"How would I know that?"

She mumbled, "Jesus." At the same time, the front door opened and greetings were exchanged in the foyer.

Hawk watched her body language and facial expressions. She was trying to look tough or bored, but she swallowed often, and her eyes blinked a bit faster than they had previously. She took two deep breaths through her nose and slowly let them out her mouth, a calming move.

As his colleagues made their way to the back of the house her eyes widened at the first two bulky figures that closed off the moonlight from the foyer and darkened the room. Even he admitted that GHOST was an impressive looking group. They all had size to them, except Jax and now Sophie. They were all badass or as they usually called Jax, badsass. And when they were together, if you didn't know them, they were downright intimidating.

Axel, then Dodge came through the door to the dining room and Roxanne's head lifted to look up at the them. Then Jax came in behind Dodge and he thought he saw her lips twitch, just a bit. If she thought she was going to intimidate Jax, she had a rude awakening coming to her.

"Roxanne, these are my colleagues, Axel, Dodge and Jax. Everyone, this is Roxanne Bowman, owner of this house."

Jax stepped forward and held out her hand. "I'm Jax. I hate babysitting."

"I'm Roxanne and I hate having my house broken into."

Roxanne's brows lifted in defiance and Jax giggled, though it wasn't a real giggle. "Well, from what we've been told, you've lied, run, and been downright uncooperative. Hawk and Wyatt could have been in and out of here if it weren't for you."

"You didn't just accuse me of holding up your damned, what did Hawk call it, 'investigation'" she used finger quotes, "when you people broke in and entered my home, in the middle of the fucking night, and might I mention, that if you'd broken in and I were still upstairs both of these giants would have been shot dead as intruders."

Jax took a step forward and narrowed her eyes, which wasn't good. "I did. We didn't break and enter anything. We were given a job and codes to do that job. And, you aren't going to get in our way. Ever. Got. It?"

Roxanne's spine straightened and Hawk decided this needed to end or they'd be scrapping on the floor soon enough. Women could be brutal when they fought.

"Okay. That's enough."

Both women continued to stare at each other as if he hadn't said anything. Clearing his throat, he repeated, "I said, that's enough."

Two beautiful heads turned to face him and if it wasn't so damned serious he'd almost laugh. These two were like polar opposites. Jax was dark-haired, dark-eyed and of Hispanic heritage and 5' 6". Roxanne had long-white-blond hair, icy blue eyes and was a few inches taller. Polar opposites. But, both tough.

"Now, this is where we're at. Roxanne, we admit we're in your house. Our contact didn't believe you'd be here tonight and told us it was safe for us to come in and look around. We're trying to find anything that will help us trace your father and mother's last days. We've accessed the official reports, but we suspect those aren't complete. We're sorry if we scared you or bothered you, but now that you know about us, we can't let you go off working this investigation on your own because you could either hamper our investigation or you could put us in a position to be found or you could get yourself hurt."

Turning his eyes to Jax he said, "Jax, we've got a mission to do and fighting with a victim isn't part of that job. Yes, things got a bit messed up with bad intel, but we've got to move on from here. I need you all to do your part. Understood?"

Jax face wrinkled, but she crossed her arms over her chest and nodded.

Kneeling in front of Roxanne again, he lowered his voice. "Roxanne, we need your cooperation. It's either that or I'm leaving Jax here to watch you while we complete our investigation. Which do you prefer?"

Roxanne's eyes darted to Jax's then back to his. She let out a breath and her shoulders slumped slightly forward. "Fine, I'll cooperate."

He reached forward and touched her knee. Mostly because he wanted to calm her, but also, he wanted to touch her. "Thank you. We promise we'll find out what happened to your parents."

Phone's began pinging and everyone dug for their phones. He remained squatting in front of Roxanne, keeping his eyes on hers, trying to convey something to her. Sincerity or confidence. Maybe it was just foolish, but he wanted her to relax. Which he shouldn't give two shits about. But for some reason he did.

Dodge said, "Gaige found an address for Raymond Bowman."

9

"**I**'m going with you." She wasn't backing down on this one. No deal would be struck, no pretending to give her something in return or 'keep her informed'. This was her idea, her deal.

Hawk took a deep breath and let it out loudly, "Look, Roxanne, it could be dangerous and..."

She stood and planted her hands on her hips. She heard a couple of snickers and remembered her clothing, but she'd deal with that later. "I'm going. If you don't bring me along, I'll get there on my own, however I have to do it. But you wouldn't have this lead if not for me. There is nothing in this house that leads my mother or father to Raymond except my father's bloodline. And you would have to go through hundreds of leads before you found Raymond. I'm going."

He stared into her eyes and she saw the instant indecision landed in his. The sun was coming up and with it, the room began filling with light. She'd been right before, his eyes were green and a gorgeous shade at that. She could see the brown flecks in them, the thick lashes that framed his almond shaped eyes and a flash of envy skittered across her mind.

"I'll give you that, it is because of you that we know about Raymond this early."

"Are you going dressed like that?"

She turned to see Jax smirking at her and it irritated her. Especially since she was right, it wouldn't work to stand out so much. Especially with this crowd. She looked around and they all wore black tactical pants, long sleeve tactical shirts and weapons. Black boots finished their clothing choices and the words flew out of her before she could check them. "I didn't bring black tactical clothing with me, but I can find something upstairs that will blend I suppose."

Jax's lips tilted up on one side of her mouth, her arms were crossed in front of her body and her head tilted to the left just enough to make her seem sort of scary in a calm, take no bullshit way. "Then let's go see. You won't be going alone up there and unless you want one of these guys with you while you dress, you're stuck with me."

Staring into the shiny brown eyes of Jax she saw the set of her jaw and stubbornness she guessed came with this woman. It was rather impressive that she could hold her own with these beasts before her.

Turning back to Hawk, she looked for his reaction and felt a bit relieved when he said, "You will do everything we tell you to do or I'll tie you up myself and leave you in the back of the vehicle. Got it?"

"Yes."

Stepping away from Hawk she faced the four colleagues who stood in her way. Lifting her brows and tilting her head she was pleased when they stood aside to allow her to pass, though Jax was closely on her heels.

She heard Hawk begin to direct the others in a plan as she made her way up the massive staircase from the foyer. Jax was silently following her but her presence was felt every step of the way.

At the top of the staircase, she walked to her bedroom and didn't even ask for a bit of privacy, she knew there'd be none. And, sadly, that was her own doing. She'd lied a couple of times so there was little use in feigning indignation. Once inside her bedroom she ground her teeth at her suitcase, which had stood in the far corner, but now lay across her bed, its contents in disarray after Wyatt likely riffled through it looking for weapons. Looking through the mess of clothing, she found a bra and matching panties, and yes, she always wore a matching set. This was nerve wracking enough without feeling out of sorts.

Finding the pair of jeans she'd brought with her, she smiled when she saw the long sleeve black t-shirt she'd initially brought to sleep in should the weather turn cold or the house feel chilly. Since they were all dressed in black, this would work.

Glancing at Jax out of her peripheral vision, she saw Jax looking over her room. Every surface, window, photograph caught her attention, as if she were memorizing every detail. Maybe if she could get her to chat, she wouldn't seem so scary.

"So, are you married?"

Slowly Jax's eyes locked with hers and froze. "I don't do girly talk unless there's a drink in my hand and my friends are with me."

"Noted."

Shimmying her 90's jeans down her legs she kicked them off to the side. Grabbing her panties, she quickly slid them up her legs and grabbed her comfy jeans from the bed, donning them without delay. Pulling her fringed top off, she tossed it on top of the bed and glanced at Jax, who once again locked eyes with her.

"Don't you know you're always supposed to check your go bag?"

"Yes, I know. I've been busy."

Slowly Jax's head shook as if she were some stupid silly girl. "Look, I get that you're all badass and working 'investigations' and used to this lifestyle. I'm not." Slipping her bra over her arms she reached back to fasten it, then continued. "I grew up here." She waved her hand around the room before snagging her long-sleeved black Tee from the bed. "I didn't live a covert life. My father spent his life in the military, and we know how to protect ourselves, shoot guns, self-defense, but living like we might have to be on the run at any given moment, I didn't live like that. So, when my dad began bugging me a few weeks ago to check my go bag, I thought it was weird, but it didn't occur to me that he thought I might actually have to use it."

She slipped her Tee over her head and tugged it down her body. Tucking it in, she looked to see Jax watching her. "I get it. I'm just giving you shit."

She inhaled and allowed the relief to settle her nerves. Reaching behind her head and pulling her braid over her shoulder, she quickly untied the band at the bottom of her braid and deftly unwound her hair. Reaching into her suitcase for her brush, she pulled it through her hair a few times, then tossed it into the suitcase.

"I can rebraid in the car if we need to get going."

"Okay, let's go then." Jax stepped back, but didn't turn her back, which she actually admired, this wasn't a stupid woman.

Snagging her phone from her bed, she stepped past Jax and descended the staircase. Color her surprised when she reached the bottom two steps and there stood four well-built, muscular, intimidating men dressed in black staring at her. The only one she really saw was Hawk, who stood a bit in front of the others and captured her eyes. Her foolish heart hammered in her chest and her cheeks flushed a bright red, if the heat in them was any indication. She still had the hair tie wrapped around her first two fingers on her right hand and she immediately began fidgeting with it.

"Stop staring at her you idiots. You've seen a woman before." Jax snapped behind her.

The men disbursed as if they'd been whipped, except for one. He wasn't as tall as Hawk and his hair was lighter in color. Stepping off the bottom step, Hawk moved aside for her to pass him, the other man stood at the railing next to the bottom step. As soon as Jax was near he said to her, "Never one so beautiful as you, Little Mama."

"Nice try, Tarzan." Jax breezed past him and headed to the door.

Hawk chuckled behind her and softly said to the blond man. "Busted."

"Shut up." Was the lighter-haired man's reply.

10

Hawk stepped to the door and said, "Okay, listen up. When Wyatt and I got here apparently there were reporters outside. They were kind enough to post it on Twitter. They, or others replacing them, might still be out there, so let's make this not so public. We also don't have to hide, though it would be nice if they didn't take pictures of our faces, so heads down, move fast, don't talk to anyone."

Opening the door, he stepped out and the others followed. Jax fell in behind Roxanne and Dodge was on her right, they effectively had her wedged in, which served a couple of purposes. First, it would be hard for her to run and second, with her white-blond hair she would no doubt be recognized, so hopefully this would shield her a little bit.

Stopping at the hedge row, he looked around as did his colleagues for signs of anyone skulking about. If reporters were here, they were well hidden. Nothing they could do about it anyway. "Go." He commanded.

They stepped between the section of hedges where the side of the drive and the end of the yard met and a small gap in the shrubbery presented itself. He stepped back and took Roxanne by the upper arm quickly leading her across the street to their rented vehicle. Axel and Wyatt drove in the second vehicle. The Beast, their fully equipped SUV was back at GHOST headquarters, so they were stuck with these babies.

A couple of weird thoughts swirled around his mind. With her long legs she kept up with his quick strides better than most and the way the sun glistened in her hair was mesmerizing. Tall and thin she looked fantastic in the jeans and long-sleeved black tee she wore now with her white-blond hair hanging down her back.

Ushering her around to the passenger side of the vehicle he opened the backdoor and helped her step up into the SUV. Sliding in behind her he said, "Buckle up."

When she twisted to pull the seat belt around her slim waist, he caught a glance of the silhouette of her breasts and once again his throat went a bit dry. It was fucking stupid.

Dodge climbed up into the driver's seat and Jax in the passenger one. He saw Roxanne look at Dodge in the rearview mirror, then over to Jax. "Roxanne, you already know Jax," he looked at Dodge, "This is Dodge. You'll hear sweet talking and see grab assing now and then. They're engaged to be married, but so far haven't set a date."

Dodge looked into the mirror and landed a look on him that seemed edgy. "Jealous?"

"No." He replied. Roxanne looked at him, her brows furrowed before she looked once again at Jax. Jax had her left arm resting on the console of the vehicle and he saw

Roxanne's eyes land on the large pink diamond on Jax's left ring finger.

The tension in the vehicle seemed thick and he was glad when Jax whispered, "Tarzan."

Dodge glanced over at her once, then started the vehicle and put it in gear. They eased from the curb and headed down the street.

Pulling his phone from his pocket, he texted his team the address. Jax immediately pulled it up on her phone setting it in the holder on the dashboard she'd brought along so Dodge had the directions in front of him.

Raymond Bowman lived at an address on the outskirts of town, and not in the nicest part of town, either. Such a huge contrast to Roxanne's family. "Why is he estranged from your family?" He asked Roxane without explanation.

She turned her head to look at him and the light blue of her eyes was entrancing as he stared into them. She was a stunning woman in so many ways. Looks, of course, she was a unique beauty with her tall, slender body, a dancer's body, and long white-blond hair. The light color of the blue in her eyes was hard to describe. Framed with long darker lashes than her hair she looked like a painting; an artist's rendition of an angel descended from heaven.

"I don't remember telling you he was estranged."

"Fair point. Why don't you know where he lives?"

"As I told you, Raymond had a high fever when he was young, and he's been off-center or not quite right in the head since. He seemed to hear voices, talk to imaginary people and lack empathy, though my mother felt otherwise. Emotion didn't show on his face, and when talking to him, people were often put off by his lack of expression. When my great-grandparents passed away, my grandpa and my great-uncle, Rowin, Raymond's father inherited their substantial estate equally. And then when my grandparents died, my dad and his two brothers, Uncle Lawrence and Uncle Lochlan were each left with sizable trust funds. As the only child, when Raymond's parents passed, he inherited. But, he didn't stay close to the family. He felt abandoned by us long ago and since he struggles with emotional attachments, he just drifted. Some in the family think he felt abandoned by us, especially his cousins, long ago. After his fever and the mental issues or whatever developed, they didn't have much to do with him.

"So, your father was his cousin, but it was your mother who tried to communicate with him?"

She took a deep breath and looked forward through the windshield. "Back when my grandparents were alive, and we had the Bonanzas she did. But after my grandparents passed and my dad and his brothers' families grew, we didn't get together that much. My uncles were also career military and stationed all over the world at any given time. Mom didn't have the time to continue to reach out to Raymond. It was exhausting I heard her tell my dad once."

"Okay. But then recently your mom said she saw him?"

"She said a man was following her who looked like Raymond. She saw him a couple of times at different locations as if he was following her. Once at a cafe where she was having lunch. Another as she was making a delivery to the hospital for wounded veterans. She said that second time she tried to talk to him, but he took off around a corner and she couldn't find him again."

She quieted and he saw her swallow and bite the inside of her cheek. Softly he asked, "Then she was killed?"

Roxanne only nodded and his heart went out to her. This was all so fresh. Her parents had only been murdered just over two weeks ago.

Dodge turned a corner, hissed out, "What the fuck is this?"

11

L ooking out the windshield to see what Dodge was seeing, she craned her neck around his shoulder.

A small white house in the middle of a block of other small houses had a squad car in the driveway and two on the street out front. The front door of the house was opened and hanging from the top hinge askew as if the home had been broken into.

Jax said, "That's our target."

"Yes." Dodge said quietly. His eyes caught hers in the mirror then he looked to Hawk. Clearly they worried that she'd fall apart or something. She wasn't going to. Not yet. Hopefully. She'd cried more in the past two weeks than she had in her whole life. Once her brothers and their families all left to go back to their homes, she'd cried for what felt like two days straight. Now, she was cried out and pissed off. Someone killed her parents and the Prime Minister of Azerbaitani and no one was being punished for it. It was either an inside job, someone was covering it all up, or the police, FBI, State Department and the White

House, were looking in the wrong direction. That was how she felt now. Someone was following her mom and she couldn't get anyone to listen to her, which was annoying as fuck.

Now, however, looking at Raymond's sad little house, the front door busted and cops swarming around, her heart hurt for him. She swallowed as two officers began unrolling the crime scene tape and wrapping it around the tree in the front yard, then to a post they had to hammer into the ground because all Raymond had was one tree in his pathetic small yard. He had money. A lot of it, why in the hell didn't he live in a nicer home in a nicer neighborhood?

Dodge pulled over to the side of the street and put the SUV in park. Turning back to Hawk he said, "You want this or someone else?"

"I've got it." Hawk responded. Turning to her he said, "You stay here and don't be trouble. I've got to go find out what's happening."

Looking at Jax, he said, "Touch base with Gaige and tell him what's going on in case we need help from Casper."

Picking up her phone from its resting place on the dash Jax began typing into it. Hawk opened the door then stopped and addressed Dodge again, "Let the others know."

He left the truck silently and so fast she blinked. For a man his size he was fast. She half-listened to Dodge and Jax following orders as she watched Hawk stride across the street and talk to the cops wrapping crime scene tape around the yard.

He was handsome in a badass dangerous way. Dark and mysterious, he said only what needed to be said, he was calculating and commanded an authority that no one questioned. Whatever organization these people worked for, at least in this time and place, he was in control. That in itself was heady and sexy. Watching his broad shoulders narrow to his waist and his ass, a mighty fine ass at that, she could see sheer power. At one point he turned and glanced at the vehicle she sat in and it was almost as if he looked right at her. Her nipples pebbled and a slight throb between her legs caused her to skip a breath. It was stupid to have that kind of a reaction to him; she still didn't even know who the hell he was but he seemed genuine. Maybe she was fooling herself to think he was anything other than a man who worked for a criminal organization who broke into people's houses after they died because they thought no one would be there. Highly plausible. Except for the codes they knew, and the fact they were helping her search for Raymond.

She rubbed her temples as she felt the beginnings of a headache begin to pound through her. Lack of sleep, lack of eating regular meals, turmoil, grief, all of it was about to catch up to her and she needed to stay ahead of it.

Jax jumped out of the passenger side of the vehicle, walked around to the hatch in the back, grabbed a large backpack and carried it to her seat in the front. Getting in and closing the door, Jax began unzipping one of the compartments. She pulled a bottle of aspirin from it, reached back and handed the bottle to her. "These should help you. Never been opened so you know I'm not poisoning you."

Jax's lips turned up into a small smile of sorts, more of a lopsided grin as she took the bottle from her. As she began opening the cap and peeling at the foil covering, she heard Jax unzip and zip a couple more openings in her backpack and she quickly handed back a bottle of water and a meal bar. "Drink this and eat the bar or you'll get an upset stomach."

She handed another bottle of water and meal bar to Dodge which earned her a genuinely beautiful smile from the man then a light kiss on the lips. Each of them began opening their meal bars without another word. So, the indomitable Jax had a soft spot for people. It made her feel less scary.

Hawk looked at the ground as the cop said something, then turned and walked back to the vehicle. Quickly feeling self-conscious she swallowed the bite of meal bar she had in her mouth and swiped her tongue around her mouth, hoping she didn't have anything in her teeth. Taking a drink of the water from the bottle Jax had given her, she quietly swished it around her mouth to cleanse it then swallowed just as he opened the door and climbed in.

"So, it appears someone was injured in or around the house. There is a small amount of blood on the ground and inside. The investigation is just beginning and Raymond is either gone or missing. No word on whether the blood is his or why the blood is there. No weapon has been discovered yet, no motive, nothing. It's something we'll need to keep our eyes on, but for now, we don't know where Raymond is. If he's in danger, a hostage, injured or on the run."

He turned to her and captured her eyes with his - the green more vibrant in this light and incredibly compelling. "Roxanne, is there anything you can think of that will help us locate Raymond? Where would he go? Who would he seek help from?"

12

H e watched her process his questions. Her eyes were intelligent, clear and held no malice that he could tell.

"I don't know. Honestly. I didn't even have his address, which begs the question, how did you get it so quickly?"

"I have contacts and I've told you, we're trying to figure out who murdered your parents, the Prime Minister and now, maybe, Raymond. Would they be connected in any way that you can think of besides Raymond being your father's cousin? Did your father maintain a relationship with Raymond?"

Her eyes darted to the house once again.

"I've got nothing. I don't feel like I've ever been here before. And, I never heard my father talking about Raymond."

"Okay, so tell me this, if we hadn't stopped in to see you today and you'd have found Raymond what would you have done when you got here?"

"I likely would have gone home and tried to figure out what to do next if this is what I'd been met with."

Both Jax and Dodge looked out the window watching as police laid down markers with numbers on them next to items in the yard.

Taking a deep breath, he ordered his thoughts to search for their next steps. "Roxanne, did the police or whoever has them give you your parents belongings or are they still holding them as evidence?"

She swallowed hard and blinked rapidly a couple of times, then he watched her gain control of her feelings and respond. "I've asked a few times. They wore formal attire and were heading to a state dinner when they were murdered. My mom's purse, phone and her favorite necklace and of course, her wedding rings are still in law enforcement custody as well as my father's uniform and medals and his phone. I'm irritated that at least the personal items haven't been returned."

"I know this is difficult," he continued, "But can you tell me how they traveled to the state dinner and what the plan for the evening was?"

She inhaled deeply and the serene look of nostalgia reflected on her face. "My parents had a limousine since Dad was Chief of Protocol for the State Department. He was the liaison for foreign dignitaries when they came to Washington. They picked up Prime Minister Mammodov from Blair House and then were driven to the White House. As they were exiting the limo, they were executed. I'm sure you have all of this in the reports from all of the law enforcement agencies."

"We do, but it doesn't hurt to go over it again from someone else's perspective. You may offer insight that the report writers don't, such as any enemies either of your parents may have had."

"Right. As far as I know, the plan for the rest of the

evening was to meet with the President, eat dinner, do the obligatory media photo op, then bring the Prime Minister back to Blair House. I don't know of any enemies my parents had."

Looking forward he said, "Jax, ask Gaige and Sophie to see if they can ping the Bowman's phones. If they can get an exact location on them, see if they can access the phones and pull down the calls over the week before the dinner, text messages, and GPS reports."

"On it." Jax replied.

Pulling up his phone, he tapped to call Wyatt's phone.

"Yeah."

"Wyatt and Axel, you two will be tracking the GPS routes once we get them. I'd like each of you to track their last locations. Visit them, take pictures and look for anything that may give us a lead.

"Jax and Dodge, you'll pour over the text messages as soon as we have them. Dates, times, locations, any encrypted or cryptic texts and anything relating to where the Bowmans and Prime Minister were, including dates and times.

"Where did your parents keep their calendars?

"Dad had a secretary on base, and his calendar synced to his phone."

He nodded. "And your mom?"

"She kept everything on her phone, too. She only kept one calendar because she didn't want to worry about missing anything."

"Okay, Jax, relay that intel to Gaige and Sophie, we'll want that information too."

"Roxanne, we can take you..."

"Nope."

"Nope, what?"

"Nope, you aren't leaving me out of this. I want to know what's going on. I've been fighting for someone to listen to me and finally it seems as though I found you, or you me, or whatever, but you aren't leaving me out of this."

Looking at Dodge in the front seat, he saw the shit-eating grin on his face. Dodge turned and looked him in the eye, his grin broadened, "Been there, done that." He said before looking at Jax which earned him a solid punch in the arm from her.

"Ouch." He rubbed his arm but the grin never left his face.

Blowing out a loud rush of air he turned back to Roxanne. "If you want to help out, you and I will look at their last phone calls, voicemails and we'll look for Leland's hard-copy calendar and track all of that data. We're working from a hotel downtown and it'll be cramped, but we'll figure it out."

Hawk turned to watch police officers for a few moments then said, "Okay, let's head to the Bowman house."

"Wait, you said..."

"We don't have the information we need to work on just yet and it could be awhile. You'll be safe at home and once I've obtained information I'll call you. Give me your phone."

She reached into her back pocket and pulled her phone out. Holding it out to him, he saw her bite her bottom lip. It wasn't meant to be sexy, but it was. He reached for her phone and she pulled it back. "Don't lie to me."

"I'm not lying." He took her phone and swiped the home screen. Needing her fingerprint to open it, he turned the phone and held it up for her. Placing her index finger on the button at the bottom of the phone, she locked eyes with him, and it sent his stomach twirling.

Her phone chimed and he turned it and found her contacts, then deftly entered his contact information. Turning the screen so she could see it, he said, "Send me a text so I have your number."

Taking her phone in her hand, their fingers brushed and his stomach twisted again. In that brief contact his thoughts went to the fact that her hands were soft.

She swallowed, then lightly cleared her throat, but he watched as her fingers tapped out a message to him. Then his phone noted a message. Looking at her lap, where a forgotten meal bar lay next to her left hand, he pulled his phone from his back pocket and read her message.

"Don't lie to me and don't leave me out."

Typing out, "I won't." He sent the message then proceeded to save her information into his phone. Without looking away from his screen he gruffly said, "Finish your meal bar."

The drive to the Bowman house was rather quiet. Jax tapped out a message on her phone and though he wanted to know who she was chatting with, he enjoyed the relative quiet. As the interior of the vehicle heated up from the rising sun, he could smell Roxanne's perfume and was surprised to find that he enjoyed it. He wasn't however, going to get used to it. He didn't have the time or the inclination to let his heart be broken again.

13

"We're here, Hawk. Driveway or garage?" Dodge asked.

Hawk replied, "Just pull in the driveway, but pull through to the back of the house. If there are reporters around, they'll have to peek through the hedges."

He turned to her, "Do you need someone to go into the house and make sure it's safe?"

She chuckled. "No, I've been going into this house for 39 years and it's always been safe until today. And, by now, our housekeeper is here, so I won't be alone anyway."

He nodded and, did he seem disappointed?

Dodge pulled into the driveway and continued on to the back of the house. The driveway was long and ran from the street, to the garage which was behind the house and lined the back street. Back in the day when this house was built, garages weren't attached to homes. And, as a matter of fact, when this house was built by her great great-grandparents, the garage was actually a stable, where the horses were housed and the carriages stored.

The vehicle stopped parallel to the backdoor and she grabbed the door handle and pulled it open. Looking at Hawk, she confirmed, "You'll call me when you have information? You promised."

"I'll call you. It may take a couple of hours for us to get the information we need. Also, if you could, do some searching in your parents' office, or their bedroom or even the basement. Anywhere they may have had hiding places for secret communications or data that might be useful. Anything that may include Raymond is a bonus."

"Okay." She opened the door and jumped out. Then thought she should be more polite. Looking directly at Jax she said, "Thanks, Jax. I appreciate your help."

To her surprise, Jax sort of smiled at her and nodded. That was it though, but she'd take it. She may be a tough nut to crack, but she'd crack it eventually. Trying to break through Jax's walls might be a nice diversion from her real life, which was getting weirder by the minute.

Closing the door she straightened her shoulders and walked to the backdoor. Entering the house into the kitchen, Carmella turned quickly and ran to her giving her a hug.

"I've been so worried. The mess all over the place looks like someone broke in. You weren't here, your suitcase is a mess. I didn't know if I should call the police. I left you four messages. I left your brothers' messages, too."

The hug felt good. Especially after the day or was it night, she'd had. So much had happened in such a short amount of time that it would take her a week to sort it all out. How was it this was her life right now?

"I'm so sorry, Carmella, I didn't mean to worry you. I was looking for a picture and then I had to run out."

"Next time leave me a clue so I don't worry. I've been wringing my hands wondering what I needed to do."

"I'm sorry. That was rude of me and if this happens again, I'll text you to let you know all is well."

"Thank you. I guess I better call your brothers and tell them everything is fine."

She hugged Carmella back. She'd been with the family for twenty-two years now and Roxanne had thought of her as a second mother growing up. When her mom was busy working, Carmella was here when she came home from school. She and her brothers were dutifully seated at the kitchen table with their homework out while Carmella made dinner for the family. But, she always fed them fresh cookies or some other tasty treat she had made for them during the afternoon. Her primary duty for the family was cleaning the house, but that had slowly morphed into cooking and she loved the family as much as they loved her.

"I can take care of it for you. I have a couple of questions to ask them anyway. Then, if it's alright with you, I need to take a nap. I've been awake since around 2:00 this morning."

"Oh, Miss Roxanne, you need to take better care of yourself. Please go rest, the vacuuming can wait until you wake up."

She gave Carmella another squeeze, then headed to the grand staircase and slowly climbed the steps to her room. Weariness set in as the comforts of home surrounded her and as she opened the door to her bedroom, tears almost sprang to her eyes. Wyatt still had her guns and her room was a mess. She'd never lived in a mess before, her parents always insisted upon clean rooms, clean clothes, everything neat and tidy. It was the military way.

Lifting her suitcase off the bed, she pushed the clothing strewn about over it, pulled the covers back and lay down. Pulling her phone from her back pocket, she typed out a message to Hawk.

"Wyatt has my guns. I'd like them back."

"I'll make sure you get them back next time we meet up." Came his response almost immediately.

A small smile tilted her lips. He'd better mean it.

She lay her phone on the nightstand and decided to nap first, then call her brothers. She'd only need a half-hour or so and then she'd feel refreshed.

The incessant ringing of a phone in the distance woke her. Her brain felt heavy and clumsy, but the ring wasn't hers. Glancing at her phone she lifted her head to see the face of it, and it wasn't lit up and ringing. It was probably Carmella's phone.

Sitting fully, she listened but the ringing stopped.

Stretching her arms high above her and arching her back she yawned then swiped her hands down her face. Turning her body and stepping from her bed, she began folding her clothing and neatly laying the items in her dresser. She'd likely be here at least a week and she hated living out of a suitcase.

Finished with the last of her clothing items, she stored her suitcase in the closet, then sat on the edge of her bed and picked up her phone.

Finding her brother, Brendan's number first, she listened as his phone rang.

"Where have you been?" Was how he answered her.

"Hi, I'm fine and thank you for worrying." She sniped back.

She heard him release a breath, then he said, "I'm sorry, Luna. I was worried when I got Carmella's message. But when I called her back, she said you'd been up since two and out of the house. So, my mind has been wandering. I've been trying to be patient for you to call me. I'm up to my ass in work here since I've gotten back."

"I didn't mean to worry you, Brendan. I'm sorry." Brendan was stationed at Camp LeJeune and had worked his way up in the ranks to full Colonel. He was responsible for 4,500 soldiers currently.

"What was so important that you were up at that hour and then out of the house?" His voice softened a bit and she detected the worry not the anger.

"Brendan, do you remember Dad's cousin Raymond?"

"Yeah, he was always more interested in video games than conversation as I recall. I think I heard Dad say a few years ago that Raymond was selling cheat codes to kids online. He spent all his time trying to crack into those games and figure them out."

Her brows bunched together. "Really? I didn't know that."

"Yeah. Dad was looking at one of Raymond's codes one day and I asked him about it. He told me he got it from Raymond to see what he was doing. That was a few years ago though, and from what I hear from my kids, they don't do cheat codes anymore."

"So you knew dad was meeting with Raymond?"

"Yeah. He touched base with him once a month I think."

She looked across the room at the door and the chair sitting in the corner next to it. The soft gray paisley pattern fit this room so perfectly. It wasn't a pattern she'd have ever chosen, but she had to admit, her mom had great style.

"I feel kind of bad that I never knew that. Did you know mom thought she saw him a few times before she died?"

She heard a chair squeak and imagined him leaning back but not getting totally comfortable. When in uniform the Bowman men didn't seek comfort.

"When did she tell you that?"

"A couple of days before they were killed."

"Why didn't you tell me when I was home?"

She crossed her legs on top of her bed, and pulled her long hair over her shoulder, running her fingers through the tangles her nap created.

"I woke up because I heard mom's voice telling me that. I guess I didn't remember it when you were here, but when you left, I called the police and tried to tell them, and they didn't want to talk to me. Actually I only told them mom thought she had a stalker. She told me he looked like Raymond. I don't know if it was Raymond or if it was someone who looked like him. They assured me they'd tell the other agencies, but I'm sure they didn't. But, anyway, she woke me up. So, I went to see Raymond at his home. But, the police were there and he wasn't. It's all so weird."

"Don't go looking for trouble, Roxanne. You need to stay safe."

"I'm safe. But, what do you think all of this means? The police won't listen to me, and I think they aren't searching in the right direction in the murder investigation. Mom had a stalker and he might lead them to the murderer or maybe he is the murderer."

His chair squeaked again and she knew he'd lurched forward and she could almost see his arms resting on his desktop, his jaw firmly set and his brows pulled together.

"Roxanne. Listen to me. Go back to work. Let the authorities handle this. I know you like digging into things and getting the answers, but these aren't your clients and this is bigger than murders. The Prime Minister of a foreign country was killed on American soil. You don't even know the shit show that is going on around it. We're getting threats here daily. Mostly from kooks and wanna-bes wanting to stir shit up. The government isn't going to leave a stone unturned."

She took a deep breath and held it until her lungs burned. Letting it out she replied, "I'm not getting involved. I just thought about Raymond and wanted to know if he was following mom."

"That's getting involved."

"Not really."

"Yes, really, it is."

"Do you know anything else about Raymond? Like where would he go if he was scared?"

"No, I don't know anything. Dad only mentioned the gaming thing to me because I saw him reading the cheat codes."

"So, Dad was still in contact with him?"

"I think it was limited contact. More like making sure he wasn't in trouble or needed anything."

"Don't you think it's odd, he didn't tell Mom."

"No, but I think it is."

Her phone beeped and she pulled it away from her ear to see her brother Matthew calling.

"Matty's calling, I better let him know I'm alright. Love you, Brendan."

"I love you too, Luna. Don't get in the way."

She ended the call and tapped the answer icon to connect her brother Matt. Brother scolding, round two, coming up.

14

His phone chimed notifying him of a text message. Glancing at the screen he read a message from Gaige.

"We've finally gotten a ping from the Bowman's phones. We're accessing now and should have data for you in about an hour."

Glancing around the rooms he was sharing with his team, Wyatt, Axel, Dodge and Jax he said, "Information coming in about an hour. Take a few minutes to eat something and rest, we may be working late."

They'd found a hotel with adjoining rooms, each with two queen beds. One nice thing about Dodge and Jax being together meant they'd always share a bed. It was easier finding rooms for an odd number this way.

He walked through the door between the rooms and lay down on the bed he'd claimed last night. They got into town late, and didn't have much sleep, so he'd take a quick nap now, which is what they were all used to doing. Sleep when you can, eat when you can because you worked at all hours.

Wyatt walked in quietly and lay down on the bed next to him, letting out a long slow breath.

Without turning his head to look at Wyatt, he said, "Roxanne wants her guns back. She isn't going to shoot us, so give them back when we see her."

Wyatt chuckled, "You got it."

He heard rustling of clothing and in the other room his comrades spoke softly but it was peaceful and relaxing. That floating feeling fell over him almost instantly.

❧

"Hawk."

His eyes flew open as he stared at Wyatt, who stood next to the bed.

"We have intel."

Sitting and swiveling his head to wake up his muscles, he immediately reached for his phone. "Okay, let's get cracking."

Wyatt walked into the other room and woke his teammates. Within just a few minutes they were all on their laptops tapping away. The information was loaded onto the servers at GHOST and stored. They'd log in and access it from wherever they were.

Entering the other room, he said, "Who's taking Leland and who's taking Kay's GPS?"

Wyatt spoke up first, "Dodge and I can take Leland's."

Axel nodded, "I've got Kay."

He looked at Jax, who sat on the bed she'd shared with Dodge, her back against the headboard, her laptop on her lap. She spoke without being asked. "I've got both of their texts. I'll set up a report and analyze them for anything that seems important."

Okay, that meant he'd have to go to Roxanne's and go over her parents' voicemails. For some reason he was both happy to work with her and resistant of the idea. He felt funny around her. Like he was worried about what she thought and how she felt, things like that. He'd managed all these years to not have those feelings for anyone. Not since caring had cost him his life. Actually the two people in this world that made his life complete. His wife, Sarah and his best friend, Colt. Since then, he'd vowed not to get involved and he'd done just fine in that department.

His phone announced a text and his heartbeat skipped when he saw Roxanne Bowman, typed on his screen.

Tapping the message icon, he read the text and his heart dropped in his chest.

"Someone broke into the house. I'm hiding in the basement in one of the storage lockers. I couldn't make it to the safe room without being noticed. Help."

"We're on our way." He typed as fast as he could. Running into the other room where his team was working away, he said, "Roxanne's in trouble. Someone is in her house and she's hiding in the basement. I may need backup."

All of them scrambled to their feet and within mere moments were running to the door. They were an impressive group.

Running down the stairs at the hotel because an elevator would be too slow right now, they expended the adrenaline rush before getting into the vehicles. They ran across the parking lot and to the SUV's and hopped in. Dodge and Jax in one, Wyatt, Axel and himself in the other. They took off without a word.

"All I got was a text, she's hiding in the basement in a

storage locker. Said she couldn't get to the safe room without being seen. So, someone is searching the house."

Wyatt began loading his guns and checking Axel's weapons to make sure while Axel drove. He rifled off a text to Roxanne. "How many?"

"Two"

Came the reply.

"Do you know who they are?"

"No"

"On our way."

Luckily Axel knew how to navigate traffic and so did Dodge, so they'd hopefully make good time. His mind wandered to Roxanne, he'd already seen her scared face this morning, he could easily picture it in his mind now. Only this time he knew without a doubt the intruders were not friendly and his heart lurched.

The rest of the ride he tried keeping his heartbeat even and his thoughts on things positive, but he couldn't stop seeing Sarah, laying in a pool of blood in front of him.

This wasn't going to end that way. They rounded the corner to the street the Bowman's lived on. "Go to the back street and park behind the garage, we'll go in through the tunnel."

Wyatt nodded his approval and chuckled. He was ready.

"Wyatt, let Dodge know to go to the front and wait for our signal."

His fingers were shaking right now, and he was still struggling to keep his thoughts even.

Easing the truck behind the garage, they silently jumped from their vehicle and he led them to the side door of the garage. The house was slightly visible from this vantage point, if you looked through the hedges. The door was locked, so he stood back as Wyatt came forward with a tool and picked the lock. Opening the door Wyatt led the group while he entered behind Axel. He closed the door as Wyatt opened the manhole cover and lowered himself into the escape tunnel.

Each in turn quietly entered the tunnel and he followed them, leaving the manhole cover open, in case they needed a quick escape. They quietly walked the tunnel, seeing the door at the end closed. Stopping at the door Wyatt listened, looked back at Hawk and shook his head.

Twisting the knob on the door, he slowly opened it and looked around. Easing himself into the room with his back against the wall Axel then Hawk followed. Axel pointed to the ceiling meaning they'd go upstairs and he nodded. He pointed to the bank of lockers and they responded. His heart was now beating even and steady, this was his game, his job and he was good at it.

They parted ways and he began searching for Roxanne. The storage lockers had windows in the upper part of the door but nothing on the bottom. She'd likely be tucked up tight to the door so they couldn't see in. Pressing his back against the wall, he pulled his phone out, and typed, "Here."

Quickly the response came back, "last room."

He looked at the bank of doors and figured the farthest from the tunnel was where she was, not knowing which door led to the safe room.

Making his way to the last door, he twisted the knob and she popped up from below it. What he saw was fear on her face and then relief.

Unlocking the door as soon as it was opened, she flew

into his arms and clung to his neck. Her shaking body pressed against his and thoughts exploded in his mind.

Whispering he said, "Do you know where they are now?"

"They went back upstairs but I don't have my guns and I thought it was stupid to follow them. And, I'm pissed at you. I want my guns back. You left me unprotected."

Shit. His stomach dropped. She was right, he'd left her unprotected. "Did you hear them speak?"

"Yes." Her breath was warm on his neck and ear, her voice shook with fear. "They are foreign. I think the language is Turkish or Iranian."

"Do you know what they were saying?"

"No, I only recognize it a bit from listening to my father as he listened to tapes from his visit there. He was preparing for the visit of the Prime Minister."

"What are they looking for?"

15

"I don't know."

He hated to do it, but he stepped back and she relaxed her hold on him. She blew out a breath and he felt sorry for her.

"Where's the safe room?" He asked.

"It's next to the tunnel."

"You need to go there, and I have to go help my team upstairs."

Just as he said that two shots rang out. He turned his head toward the steps but hesitated. Looking at Roxanne, he said, "Go to the safe room."

She nodded and he headed to the stairs. He watched as she scooted across the room and twisted the knob on the door next to the tunnel. He then went upstairs quietly.

At the top of the steps he saw a woman in her 50's, sitting on the kitchen floor, a gag in her mouth and her hands and feet tied. The fear in her green eyes was evident. He looked at her and held his finger to his lips asking her to be quiet. He saw her swallow and close her eyes. Looking around the door jamb toward the dining room he pressed his back to the wall. Glancing again at the woman he saw her eyes look toward the other side of the kitchen and knew she was trying to help him.

Walking to the open basement door, he looked around it and saw the back of a dark-haired male head looking toward the foyer. His gun was pointed at someone and he was frozen in place. Hawk pulled his weapon and held it up in front of him, pointed at the man. The man turned and saw him and trained his weapon on Hawk, but was shot from the side by one of his team.

Shock registered on his face as he slowly realized he'd been shot. Then he turned to his shooter, but fell to his knees. He'd been shot in the ribs from his right side, a small spot of blood on his shirt could be seen, but only one. That meant the bullet was still inside him. His breathing began to turn to a wheeze indicating he'd been shot in the lung.

Wyatt stepped into the room and nodded to him, turned back to the assailant and yelled, "Drop your weapon."

Still pointing his gun at the intruder his eyes locked tight on the man. Hawk stepped into the room slowly, the man's weapon wobbled as he held it, then his grip loosened but he still hadn't dropped it and you never trusted he wouldn't raise it and shoot.

Axel stepped into the living room behind Wyatt, his gun drawn and trained on the man on his knees. The man raised his gun swiftly to under his chin and shot himself in the head.

Watching in what felt like slow motion as his gun fell from his hand, his body slowly slumped over and fell to the ground. Blood spattered the carpet in front of the sofa and on the sofa and coffee table. Axel stepped forward and kicked the gun away from the man, even though he was likely dead after that, you couldn't be too sure.

Finding his voice, Hawk said, "the other one?"

"Dead. Dodge got him in the office."

"Call it in."

They'd have to deal with the local police on this but if they needed assistance, they could call Casper.

He turned to the kitchen to untie the woman sitting on the floor but found Roxanne untying her instead.

"You're supposed to be in the safe room."

"I couldn't get the door open."

"How is it a safe room door can't be opened? It doesn't seem very safe."

She finished untying the scared woman then stood and looked him in the eye. "It's like its locked from the inside. I don't know what's up with it."

"Is someone in there?"

Her brows furrowed and she shook her head. "Who would be in there?"

"Do you have a key or a safety unlock just in case?"

The woman who had been tied up stood. He guessed her height at 5'5" or so, shorter than Roxanne and certainly shorter than himself. Her dark hair was tied up in a bun at the top of her head, but she squared her shoulders and rubbed her wrists. She hugged Roxanne and whispered something in either Spanish or Italian, he wasn't sure which and he couldn't hear the words clearly, but Roxanne replied, "I'm okay, Carmella, are you?"

"Oh, yes."

"Carmella, this is Hawk. He and his team were hired to help find out who murdered Mom and Dad and the Prime Minister." Turning to him, her crisp blue eyes no longer held the fear they'd had in them previously, her face had relaxed somewhat from moments ago when she'd thrown herself in his arms. "Hawk, this is Carmella, our housekeeper and my friend. She's been with my family for twenty-two years now."

The older woman smiled at him but it was a wary smile, it didn't reach her eyes and she remained rooted in place. Stepping forward, he held his hand out to her.

"I'm pleased to meet you, Carmella."

She hesitantly took his hand in hers and shook, but pulled back quickly and folded her hands together in front of her stomach. Nodding once she then put her arm around Roxanne's waist and hugged her close.

Roxanne wrapped her right arm around Carmella's shoulders and squeezed her tight. After a few moments he asked both women, "Is there a key or a safety release to get into the safe room?"

Carmella nodded her head, "Yes sir, Mr. Hawk. Mr. Bowman had the only other one in the house."

She then looked at Roxanne until Roxanne bobbed her head once.

Carmella walked to the far end of the cabinets, pulled open the bottom drawer and removed the kitchen towels from inside, laying them on the counter. Once everything had been removed, she pushed firmly on the bottom of the drawer and the bottom popped up a half-inch, enough for Carmella to get her fingers around the edge and pull it up. The false bottom was lifted out and an envelope was pulled from it. Carmella handed the envelope to Roxanne, who proceeded to tear it open and dropped a silver key into the palm of her hand.

16

———

Hawk held his hand out for the key, but this was her home and if someone was in the safe room, she wanted to be the first person to see them; which, now that she thought about it, meant she'd need her gun.

Stopping at the doorway to the basement she squared her shoulders and tipped her head back to look at Hawk. "I want my guns back."

"If you're scared, Roxanne, I can go down there."

"It would be stupid to say I wasn't a little bit nervous, but I do want my guns back. Now would be a great time."

His eyes searched hers for a long time. It wasn't all that unpleasant looking into his. The green was something akin to a bright olive which stood out even more against his dark olive skin tone. His irises were ringed with a deeper green. His black hair was worn combed back from his face but she could tell it was thick. Where the sunlight streamed through windows touched it, it gleamed.

Without looking away from her, he called, "Wyatt?"

"Yeah?" Wyatt responded.

Soon footsteps came closer to their location and a low chuckle sounded. "Princess want her guns back?"

Finally, she broke eye contact with him and addressed Wyatt. "Yes, I want my guns back."

He unzipped a pocket halfway down the right leg of his tactical pants and pulled out her 9mm, which was the gift from her father. From his other pant leg, he did the same and pulled her 380 out. Holding both of them, muzzle down, he extended his arms and she gently took both guns from his hands. Quickly tucking her 308 in the back of her jeans waistband, she dropped the clip on her 9mm, checked that it was full of bullets, slid it back in and checked that it was secure. Then she loaded a bullet into the chamber of her gun, turned and began descending the steps to the basement.

Wyatt chuckled again and mumbled, "Badass."

Hawk's steps were directly behind hers and she'd be lying if she said she was unhappy about that. Honestly, not knowing what or who was in the safe room was a bit creepy to say the least.

At the bottom of the steps she turned left and walked across the sitting area set up there. The oversized brown leather sofa sat against the wall to her right, two recliners of matching leather faced the sofa. A simple oak coffee table was placed in front of the sofa and she smiled when she saw it. Her brother Matt had made that in shop class his junior year in high school.

The safe room door was directly in front of her on the far wall. The four-panel door was identical to all the other doors down here and stood next to the tunnel door. Opening the four-panel door showed another door, made of metal with a keypad on it. Just below the keypad was the lock override where the key could be inserted. She tried the code once again, the six digits ingrained in her brain from the time she was very little and her grandparents lived here. 751571. She never knew the significance of the code or if there was importance to it.

The door opened and she jumped. With a whoosh, she pushed it inside and Hawk quickly stepped in front of her, which only flashed her anger for a millisecond before gratefulness flooded her mind, she lowered her gun so the muzzle was facing the floor.

Two steps down into the room he walked and stopped. The lights clicked on automatically and she heard him mutter something. Stepping down into the safe room, she looked around in disbelief. Someone had been here alright. The first of two double bunk beds was unmade, an MRE package lay on top of the garbage basket and a half-full glass of water sat on the table next to the bed.

Several sheets of paper lay on top of the disheveled bed coverings. Hawk looked around the room, his gun at the ready. She watched his movements and had to admit he was impressive. The tight black t-shirt he wore stretched across massive back muscles and showed the definition of his finely fit body. The myriad of tattoos on both arms were interesting and fit his personality. Slowly he walked over to the kitchen area, which was simply across from the two sets of bunk beds. There was enough room for their whole family should they need it. The sofa which stood behind the open door also pulled out to a sleeper, if needed, but was not now pulled open.

Looking across the room there was a door against the far wall. "Where does that go to?" He asked.

"It's a small bathroom."

Slowly making his way silently across the room, he quickly jerked open the door and held his weapon in front of him. The light clicked on and his eyes and gun swept the room. Satisfied that no one was inside, he backed out and closed the door. Tucking his gun into the holster at his waist, he walked to the bed and picked up the papers laying there. His eyes scanned the sheets, one at a time and he slowly shook his head.

Holding the papers out to her he asked, "Do you know what this means? It looks like code."

Taking the papers from him she scanned them which was a series of letters in small bits. Tcl, tic, tm first check FO4-3. The second sheet of paper held other codes beginning with 890 pearls, console key = 200 - LoG. The other pages held similar codes on and on. Her stomach turned as the thoughts that this was likely written by someone who'd had a mental break with reality had been here. In her home. And had the codes to get in.

Swallowing she responded. "It looks like code, but nothing I've ever seen before certainly nothing that makes any sense."

Hawk turned and opened the drawers under the counter in the kitchen area then closed them. Same with the cabinets. She looked around the room as well, willing her mind to find something that would make sense of all of this.

"Who has access to this home and especially this room?"

"My brothers and I."

He moved toward her slowly, his eyes locked on hers, "Raymond?"

"No." Swallowing she added. "Who would have given him the code to get in here? He likely knew about the tunnel because his father, my great-uncle Rowin and my grandfather, Derren, were brothers. They grew up in this house and then grandpa lived here for years after. Rowin and his family moved to their newer home just out of the city. It's likely the family would have known this safe room was here. Back in the day when there was so much chatter about the Russians dropping nuclear weapons on us, my grandfather fortified this room, and the tunnel was reinforced. That was before I was born. Though once electronics were more common, my father had it upgraded again, and I can't picture him sharing the code with anyone outside the family. At least not without telling us."

"What about your dad's best friend?"

She inhaled deeply to keep her fears at bay. That brought his scent into her lungs though and goosebumps raised on her arms. "I think it's safe to say at this point that I simply don't know."

"Okay. At this point we know someone was in here and we can assume it was Raymond, but we can't be sure. But, Raymond's house was broken into, he's in the wind as far as we know, and at least at this point, he's the only one who possibly has the code and needs a place to hide. That being said, I'm calling this into headquarters and we'll discuss telling local law enforcement."

Her arms hung down, a gun in her right hand, her left hand fisted. Hawk gently lay his right hand on her shoulder and when she tilted her head up to look at him, his hand moved to the side of her neck, his thumb softly brushed across her cheek. "Let's take these sheets of paper upstairs and lock this room up until we can figure out what this code means. Then, we need to figure out where you're going to stay, because you can't stay here alone."

She felt that way as well, but she didn't have any other place to go, except her home which was a 90 minute commute on a good day. That was too far to be able to figure things out.

The thought of a hotel seemed like too much trouble at the moment and what about Carmella?

"So, don't make me regret this, but there's plenty of room, why don't you set up operations here? I won't be alone, we can monitor this room and block the tunnel from anyone getting in or out, which also limits our movement somewhat."

He chuckled slightly, "Why would you want us in your home?"

"Because then I'll be here and can be involved and you won't be hiding information as easily from me. And, maybe together we'll all be able to figure out this puzzle about my parents' murders that keeps getting more and more confusing."

"Roxanne, I don't know if you know what you're saying. We work around the clock sometimes. Then there are other times when we don't do anything for a long time, if we're waiting for information or permission to move forward."

"Hawk, it makes the most sense. This house is huge, there's plenty of room. And I don't feel safe alone right now, but I would if you all were in the house. Plus, clearly, someone wants something that they believe is here. You did, too."

Commotion upstairs caught her attention and her stomach twisted. There were dead men upstairs and that thought was sickening.

"Local PD is here and I have to handle this. You can stay here if you like."

"No, I'm going up with you. Carmella may need some comforting and the police will need my statement."

"Until I get the okay to include law enforcement in this situation down here, don't say anything about it."

"So, you want me to lie?"

She watched his face harden but his eyes bore into hers. "Just by omission. At least for now. If they start crawling around here, they might clue whoever else thinks there is information here that we've found something. That could make things more deadly. Our contacts can liaison between our team and law enforcement, until we have something."

17

Sitting at the dining room table in the impressive Bowman home, Hawk looked at his team, all of them with laptops opened and working on their respective tasks. Wyatt and Axel were mapping out Leland and Kay Bowman's last GPS routes the month before they were killed. Jax and Dodge were looking over the Bowman's text messages and outlining dates, times, messages and to whom those messages were to or from. Roxanne was to his right, on her laptop looking at her mother's phone records and entering the information into the spreadsheet he'd downloaded for her from their GHOST system. He could then upload it to their servers and it would be entered into their software to locate similarities, patterns, dates and times that coincided with other important data and their calendars; it served its purpose as to Roxanne's knowledge and didn't reveal anything about GHOST.

The local PD had left a couple of hours ago. Casper had made some phone calls or had someone else make them, either way, local PD worked efficiently and didn't give them a lot of grief. They took the bodies away, the living room and the foyer were still crime scenes of sorts, the white carpeting and sofa had been removed from the house by the police, after numerous photographs, measurements and data were taken and Carmella was overseeing replacements at Roxanne's request. His phone rang. Snagging it off the table next to his computer he read the name on his screen, tapped the answer icon and held the phone to his ear.

"Gaige, what did you find out?"

"So, the two men your team found today, who had intruded into the Bowman home, are citizens from Azerbaitani. Both had just recently entered the country. Airline records show one of them entering three days after the Prime Minister and the Bowmans were killed and the second, two days after that."

"Revenge for their Prime Minister or was Leland Bowman the target of the murders?

His eyes darted to Roxanne; who's eyes darted to his the instant her father's name was mentioned. She swallowed then slowly dropped her hands to her lap.

"They didn't have time to take anything from the Bowman residence before your team stopped them, but they were there for a reason."

"Right. They must have thought something was here. They focused on Leland's office, which is where we found one of them. We'll search the office further and the house."

"Good luck. I'll be in touch in a bit. Out."

"Out."

He lay his phone alongside his computer. Five pair of eyes stared at him, waiting for their next orders.

"The intruders were from Azerbaitani. They came to

Washington for a reason." He looked into Roxanne's eyes. "Would your father keep information here? Personal information he gathered on the Prime Minister? Azerbaitani? Or someone else associated with either of them? Someone seems to think he may have."

When she responded her voice was surprisingly calm. "He has a room downstairs that he kept his work in. We were never allowed in there. My mom went in there once in a while, but mostly it was a place where Dad stored things when he was working on a big project, learning about the countries about to visit, its customs, foreign policy with us. Things like that."

"And no one asked for the key while they were investigating?"

"Not that I'm aware of. My brother, Brendan, handled most of that. I can call him."

"Okay, give him a call. In the meantime, where did Leland keep the key?"

"It was always on him. He had a keyring he never let out of his sight. It had some keys to his office at work, the key to his storage room in the basement and the safe room override. I haven't gotten those keys back from the law enforcement agencies yet. They should still be with my father's things at the morgue or wherever they are storing them."

He looked up and Axel was already closing the lid on his laptop and ready for action. Networking and surveillance were his specialties. Axel stood up and met his gaze, a crooked grin on his face.

"We need the exact location of Leland's keys, which should be in close proximity to his phone. We have that on the system." He nodded to his laptop.

Axel looked at Roxanne and though he looked sorry

he had to ask, he forged ahead. "Roxanne, with all you have set up here in this house, don't you have a security system in place?"

"Yes, we do, but I don't have it engaged." Her brows furrowed together.

"Why on earth not?" Jax crossed her arms over her chest and the look of irritation on her face was crystal clear. Roxanne looked across the table at Jax and said, "During the day when Carmella and I are both in the house, we don't turn it on. Otherwise we inadvertently set it off when we walk outside for a minute, or one of us leaves for groceries or errands."

He leaned forward and softly said, "You didn't have it engaged last night, either. Wyatt and I were able to get into the house without a sound."

"I've never felt unsafe here. I've never been scared. Last night and today I've been freaked out more than I have been in my whole damned life. So, I just don't think about it. I will from now on though."

Axel nabbed his laptop from the table and stepped back. "What about video surveillance? Do you have cameras installed around the perimeter?"

"Yes, those are accessed with my Dad's computer." She pushed her chair back then stood but hesitated at taking a step. Running her fingers over the bridge of her nose she quietly said, "I don't know where Dad's laptop is. My best guess is it's in the storage room downstairs or at his office on base. Mom said he'd been especially secretive recently. This Prime Minister's visit seemed of the utmost import to him."

"Axel, you and Wyatt need to figure out a way to get the keys. Call Gaige and have him call Casper if need be."

"On it." Axel said.

Wyatt stood, closed the lid on his laptop and snagged it from the table. Turning to move past his chair he stopped mid-motion and turned to Roxanne. "Why was he more secretive lately than other times?"

He turned his head and watched her face. Her beautiful, petite face with the pale blue eyes that reminded him of a moonstone they were so light. Slightly shaking her head, she responded, "I don't know. She asked him a few times and he just told her it was Department matters."

He watched her closely and didn't detect that she was lying. He could always spot a liar. Their eyes always shifted, they fidgeted, some telltale sign that they weren't comfortable with themselves in that moment. Roxanne answered questions and genuinely seemed as puzzled as they all were.

Dodge said, "Well look here. Leland got a text message three days before he was killed that's rather cryptic. "I'll meet you at the usual. RB. Could that be Raymond Bowman?"

18

Why on earth would her father have been in contact with Raymond? She didn't think that he had had a relationship with Raymond at all, until this afternoon when Brendan mentioned her father checking on him a few years back, but it appeared he had held secrets and her stomach twisted at the thought that her father may have been involved in something untoward. He'd always been up high on a pedestal as far as she and her brothers were concerned. But now nothing seemed as it had before. Her life was unraveling at breakneck speed.

First thing on the agenda was to call Brendan. After that she'd see what this team of people were up to, whoever they were. She looked at Hawk and was relieved when he simply nodded. Closing the lid on her laptop she stepped away from the table and slowly walked to the staircase. She avoided looking into the living room and her parents' office for the time being. She didn't need to be reminded again of what had just transpired there.

Her legs felt heavy and each step felt like a monumental climb, but she could do this. At the top of the steps she walked to her bedroom door stepped inside the room, and softly closed the door behind her. Leaning against the closed door she let her head rest back on the wood, closed her eyes, took in a few deep breaths letting them out slowly.

After allowing herself a few moments of pity she sat on the edge of her bed, pulled her phone out of her pocket, and scrolled for Brendon's phone number. Tapping his picture on her phone, she held it to her ear and listened as it rang.

"Hey Roxanne, what's up?"

"Brendan, did anyone from the military ask you for Dad's keys to his room in the basement?"

"No, why do you ask?"

"Okay well I have a few things to tell you starting with the house being broken into today."

Forty minutes later she felt rung out, totally exhausted. Brendon had been upset naturally, and answering his questions, especially after all the questions Hawk and his group had asked, the day felt more like a week. The only interesting information she'd gotten from that phone call was that her father had had a relationship with Raymond. Though even Brendan didn't know how close they were, what he did know is that their father had met Raymond once a month or so for coffee. How is it she never knew that? Her mother never said a word to her about it either. She needed to find Raymond because things kept pointing to him and the more she thought about it now, the more sense it made that it was Raymond who had been in the safe room. Maybe he'd come back, since his house was a crime scene now, for whatever reason; though he was likely afraid to come back to her house because of all of the people around.

Standing and stretching her arms out in front of her she enjoyed the feeling of stretching her back muscles. Her neck had stiffened as the day drew on and she wasn't used to all this sitting. Tucking her phone into the back pocket of her jeans she started toward her bedroom door when her phone rang. Quickly pulling it from her pocket she saw Brendan's name on her phone. Inhaling deeply to prepare herself for another onslaught of questions she let her breath go and tapped the answer icon.

"Hey Brendan."

"Roxanne, I just got a letter in the mail. Sent here to the base. No return address on it and not any handwriting I've ever seen before. I called Dad's friend, Wade, and he told me to send it to a Hawk. Says he's staying in the house. I think there are a few things you left out of our phone conversation."

"I told you some people were here to help and were hired by someone to find the person or people responsible for killing Mom and Dad. And the Prime Minister."

"You didn't tell me they were staying in the house. With you."

She plopped down onto her bed once again in exasperation. "That was a recent development. After those men broke into the house, and they had to be killed or Carmella and I might have been, I asked them if they'd like to stay. To be honest, I'm a little creeped out now and having a house full of people calms my nerves a bit. Plus, they have all sorts of government access Brendan and the equipment they have is first rate. They're working hard to figure out this mess."

"Who hired them?" His voice took on that military command tone and she winced.

"I don't know. They said they can't tell me."

"I'll bet it was Wade, he seems comfortable with them and knew instantly what I should do with the letter. But, I think I'll see if I can manage another leave and come home to see what the hell is going on."

"Brendan, don't go getting everyone riled up. I feel safe for the time being."

"Where is this Hawk now?"

"He's downstairs in the dining room with his team."

"Take your phone down and let me talk to him."

"Bren..."

"I mean it, Roxanne. Do you know how freaked out I am being so far from home and all this shit going on? Don't test me. Not now."

She inhaled a deep breath and stood from her bed, listening on her phone in case Brendan said anything else to her, but she knew from his tone, he was about to lose his shit and now wouldn't be a good time to argue with him.

Exiting her bedroom, she quietly walked down the staircase, averting her eyes away from the living room as she reached the bottom step. Turning to her right she walked to the dining room from the foyer and as soon as she entered the room conversation stopped. The only people left in the room were Hawk, Jax and Dodge, but whatever they'd been discussing ended. Twisting her head from side to side to ease some of the tension she walked straight to Hawk and held out her phone.

"My brother Brendan would like a word."

He held her gaze for a long moment and she saw the concern in his green eyes. His brows furrowed slightly, but he regained all composure and gently accepted her phone.

"Hawk Delany here."

She resumed her seat at the table and to Hawk's right and tried to listen for anything she might be able to hear. She glanced at Jax who was watching her, a lopsided grin on her face. Not knowing Jax that well, she wasn't sure if she was getting a kick out of the fact that Brendan was likely chewing Hawk out or something else. Jax didn't yammer on and on about things, that was for sure. She was a hard one to read.

Hawk said, "Text me pictures of the letter and overnight me the original and I'll see what I can find out about it."

19

His phone chimed that a text had been received. Opening the text he scanned the brief message. "Here you go." is all it said. Clicking on the attachment he opened the picture and scanned the letter. It looked like the same code in the papers they had found in the basement.

He said to no one in particular. "Whoever was in the basement either sent a letter to Brendan or is in cahoots with the person who did send the letter. It's the same type of code. I'm forwarding a copy to each of you".

Clicking the send button all of their phones immediately chimed. He watched them open the texts and glance at the attachment including Roxanne.

Her nose wrinkled for a moment, then her face took on her stoic facade. She was good, he'd give her that, but he could see the thrumming of her heart in the pulsing in her neck and it was beating rapidly. Her right hand raised and rubbed the back of her neck. She rotated her head a bit and he could tell stiffness had set in. All the stoicism was taking its toll on her.

Carmella came into the dining room and said, "Dinner is ready. You'll either need to set your computers aside or stand with your plates in your hands, your choice." She turned and walked back into the kitchen.

Jax giggled. "I like her."

Closing the lids on their laptops they each tucked them into their respective cases and one by one left the room for the kitchen. He and Roxanne were alone in the room for a moment, and he asked, "Are you okay? If you need to lie down, please do. Once we're finished pouring over these data records, we'll upload them to our server and find commonalities so we'll have some downtime."

She smiled at him and at first it was as if someone sucker punched him. She was stunning before, even when angry. But this sweet, smiling, vulnerable Roxanne was incredible. His stomach tightened and his heart hammered. Her eyes stared into his for long moments before she said anything. He saw her swallow then softly she said, "I'll be fine until bedtime. It's just been a long day and one the likes of which I've never encountered."

Her left hand lay on the table between them and he couldn't stop himself from the need to touch her. Laying his hand over hers, he swallowed the lump that formed, then said, "We're here for you and you're safe now."

Her hand turned in his and she locked her fingers with his. His heart pounded in his chest and his throat dried instantly. She squeezed his hand in hers, her smile widened and she said, "I feel very safe with you all here and I can't thank you enough."

She stood and he was frozen in place. He hadn't had these feelings since...since he'd met his wife, Sarah. Since that time, he'd done a damned good job of not letting himself fall in love. He didn't want to risk his heart - ever again. It was too painful when it went bad. Especially when he was the reason she was no longer with him.

He watched Roxanne walk to the kitchen. Her long platinum hair cascading down her back and oddly bright against the dark t-shirt she now wore. The jeans she had on encased her shapely ass perfectly and his fingers twitched of their own accord. He fisted his hand and closed his eyes. He couldn't let himself fall for the gorgeous Roxanne Bowman. He couldn't risk his heart and her life. He just couldn't.

"What's wrong with you?" Jax asked as she set her plate, filled with delicious smelling food, on the dining room table and took her seat."

"Nothing."

He stood and she chuckled. "Really? 'Cause it looks like you're sweet on Roxanne and trying not to be."

"I am not. It doesn't look like that."

"Suit yourself, big guy."

"Suit himself what?" Dodge asked as he sat next to Jax.

"Hawk doesn't want to admit he's kinda sweet on Roxanne."

Dodge laughed. "Doesn't have to admit it, we can all see it anyway."

"Shut the fuck up. It's not like that. I just want to do a good job." He snapped.

As Dodge and Jax smiled and nodded their heads he stomped out to the kitchen so he didn't have to hear any more of their bullshit.

The basement door opened and Axel and Wyatt entered the kitchen.

Wyatt took in a deep breath. "Damn, it smells fantastic in here."

Axel sidled up to the stack of plates on the counter

and Wyatt was right behind him. Grabbing plates, they began loading up on the food Carmella had prepared for them. A fresh ham, mashed potatoes, green beans, jello salad, fresh buns and real butter. He hadn't eaten like this in a long time. Kylie and Mrs. James, at GHOST headquarters, were great cooks, but they made healthy meals, nothing like this spread.

Roxanne walked into the dining room with her plate of food and he couldn't stop watching her.

Wyatt broke into his thoughts. "We got the keys."

"How did that happen?"

"Gaige called Casper and Casper called someone else, who met us at the door with the keys in an envelope."

"Nice. As soon as we're finished eating, we'll head down to the storage room and see what we can find."

"Who's Casper?" Roxanne stood in front of her chair, her plate on the table, her arms crossed in front of her.

"He's a contact we have."

"And he works on base?" The suspicion in her voice was clear.

"No, he doesn't exactly work on base. We have contacts."

"What are you some undercover organization?"

Wyatt, Axel and he stopped filling their plates and stared at Roxanne from the kitchen. Wyatt was the first to respond. "We've told you, we aren't at liberty to divulge that information. You can be a part of this as long as you don't pry. If and that's a big if, we get permission to tell you who we are, who we work for, then we'll fill you in. Or Hawk will. But until that time princess, no questions along those lines, comprende?"

Her eyes narrowed as she looked at Wyatt. They had a stare down for a few moments and Axel decided that was enough. "Okay folks, let's eat before this gets cold, we may have a long night ahead."

Axel walked into the dining room and Wyatt followed. Roxanne's eyes slid to his and locked. "Is your agency an illegal agency?"

"We're not illegal. We're just not...on the radar."

20

Not on the radar. The plot thickened yet again. Her mind raced for anything to grasp what that meant. They didn't seem as though they were on the wrong side of the law and Wade seemed to trust them. Her phone chimed and she pulled it off the table next to her where Hawk laid it down before going to get his own plate of food.

Brendan texted. *Just got off the phone with Wade again. This group is good. He won't say more, but they'll keep you safe. Love you.*

She quickly replied. *Thank you. Love you too.*

She lay her phone back on the table next to her plate on the left and began nibbling at her food. It smelled amazing, but she wasn't the least bit hungry. She'd seen two men shot to death in her childhood home today. Carmella tied up. Strangers break in and think she was a burglar. Had her escape thwarted by said strangers and someone had access to the safe room. That was all on top of the fact that her father seemed to have been involved in something rather unusual and maybe even worse, criminal or on the outside of the law with all the secrets he'd held. And, back to the beginning, her mom was sure she had a stalker who looked like Raymond and then both her parents had been killed. Lastly, where the hell was Raymond.

Taking a deep breath, she lay her fork on the side of her plate and stared at the food on her plate.

She felt the second Hawk entered the room. It was as if there was an electric current pulling at her hair and skin when he was near. Her body sensed his presence and responded in the weirdest way. She'd never had an attraction to a man like this before and it seemed wholly scary and made her feel out of control.

Closing her eyes she counted as she controlled her breathing. Inhale and count to ten. Exhale to the count of ten. Repeat. Hopefully she'd turn in early tonight. A good night's sleep would certainly help her get her mojo back.

"You need to eat."

Hawk's deep voice softly admonished her and her nipples pebbled. Damn it.

"I'm just not that hungry. I'm sure tomorrow will be a new day and I'll be back to my old self again."

She tried not looking into his eyes. She got lost every time she did. Chalking it up to being tired and out of sorts made her feel a bit better. That's what she told herself anyway.

"You can go up and get some sleep now if you like. We'll likely not do much more tonight once we upload our intel into the server, I'll upload yours. We'll need to wait for compatibles to come back and that can take a few hours. We'll all likely get some shuteye during that time."

Lifting her eyes to his, she saw sincerity and honesty. "I

want to go downstairs and see what's in my father's room first."

His nod was so slight she almost missed it. Then he began eating his food and it seemed as though he forgot she was there. The others chatted about nothing in particular. The weather. Something they saw on the road.

Then Wyatt asked, "When are you two finally getting married? We're due for a party."

Jax sat back in her chair and looked at Dodge. It was beautiful watching them together. The way she looked at him softened her normally badass demeanor. His face changed when he looked at her, too. Then he looked at his friends and said, "As soon as we get back home, we're getting married. No big shindig, just all of you and immediate family."

Wyatt spoke first. "Well, what makes you two think we all want to be there?"

Jax gave him the finger and Dodge chuckled. "You fuckers will be there."

Axel chuckled, his longer dark hair covered a scar that ran the length of the right side of his face. She'd seen it earlier today and wanted to ask about it, but couldn't bring herself to do it. "I'll be there. And I'll be thirsty."

Dodge laughed and shoveled a forkful of mashed potatoes into his mouth. Jax continued eating as well but Roxanne still didn't have an appetite. Glancing at Hawk revealed him watching her again and her cheeks flushed a crimson if the heat was any indicator. She swallowed and tried to ignore the butterflies in her belly and the dampness that gathered between her legs. He nodded once again, then pushed his plate toward the center of the table. Within just a few seconds Wyatt and Axel did the same.

Carmella came in to remove their plates just as Jax and Dodge finished their meals and Hawk said to the group. "Ready to investigate the contents of Leland's room downstairs?"

Wyatt was first to jump up, clap his hands and enthusiastically say, "Yep. Let's do this."

Hawk stood and she followed his lead as each of the other team members stood, grabbed phones from the table and pocketed them with ease. They'd definitely done this before; their movements were fluid.

Hawk stepped away from his place at the table and with his right hand, ushered her between him and the table and past the others to the basement door. She could feel him close behind her and she was glad no one else could see her face. With her fair coloring even, the slightest blush was obvious.

Once she reached the basement door, she hesitated only a second before pulling the door open and beginning her descent. The myriad of footsteps behind her told her they were all coming down, as if this were the big moment of the day - not the men they'd killed earlier. Walking through the sitting area, she turned to the left and stopped in front of her father's door. Her heart beat so fast it felt like it would jump from her chest and she swallowed and inhaled to steel herself for whatever they'd find. For the first time in her entire life, she worried the man she'd known and loved had not been the man she'd thought he was and that scared her more than anything that had transpired today.

Hawk stepped up next to her with the key in his hand and easily inserted it into the lock. Turning the key to the left and twisting the doorknob, he opened the sanctuary she'd never set foot in.

The lights flicked on, the bluish glow from the cold florescent lamps washing the room in an eerie blue-gray color. A medium-sized wooden desk, smaller than the desk upstairs, sat in the middle of the room, facing toward the door, and bookshelves lined the three walls on either side and behind it. As the bulbs from the lamps warmed and washed the room in a brighter light, she cautiously entered her father's domain and glanced at the books.

The shelves to the left of the door held many three ring binders, mostly black, but a few blue and green ones scattered throughout. There were only cryptic acronyms on the spines and two or three digits after. She glanced at the entire wall of shelves with not a clue to what any of it meant.

Slowly turning to look at the wall opposite, she saw Hawk and his team watching her from the doorway. Glancing at him briefly, then to the shelves behind him she softly said, "I've never been in here."

21

Looking at her from this vantage point, you'd suspect she was fragile. She was anything but. While she was tall and thin, she held her shoulders straight, probably that military kid upbringing. Her pale skin, silvery-white hair and light blue eyes instantly made a person think nymph or fairy. But, she held a gun in one hand and had one tucked in her jeans and she didn't shy away from coming down here with them, in fact, she insisted on being first.

He gave her a few minutes to assess the room, then cleared his throat. "Roxanne, we have to get to work."

Her eyes landed on his and held briefly before she responded. "What do we need to do first?"

Relief flooded through his system that she wasn't going to break down. She was strong. Impressively strong.

"Dodge and Jax, take pictures of everything before we touch or move anything. In case there's a rhyme or reason to the order of these books, we need to be able to recreate it."

Turning to Roxanne he said, "Once they're finished with the pictures, we'll begin searching the desk. We're looking for his laptop, perhaps another one, a cell phone or a burner phone, and any paperwork regarding Azerbaitani, blackmail notes, or threatening messages regarding your mom or any of your family members."

Her brows furrowed momentarily, then she slowly nodded her head. "Because of my mom's stalker." It wasn't a question, so he didn't answer.

Cameras could be heard clicking behind him as Jax and Dodge moved throughout the room, snapping at every surface.

He walked behind the desk. The only items on the top were a small desk lamp, a black desk pad, a black stapler and a black tape dispenser. Neat, clean and orderly.

Dodge came to stand beside him, and Hawk stepped back to allow Dodge the room to open each drawer in turn and snap pictures of the contents. Dodge opened, snapped and closed each drawer. When he was finished, Dodge tapped a few icons on his phone, then nodded. "Upload complete."

Beginning with the top middle drawer Hawk pulled the handle and once again revealed the contents inside. Smaller cubes organized the inside of the drawer, carefully sorting pens, paperclips, rubber bands, a ruler, lead for a pencil, a box of staples and additional rolls of tape. Nothing out of place.

Starting at the right he opened the top drawer and only found a narrow ledger book. Pulling it from the drawer he lay it on the desktop and slowly opened it. Inside revealed what looked to be the household finances. Electric, gas, telephone, maintenance, payroll, etc. Each page was dedicated to a month and year, in perfect succession. The last entry was the day before he died.

As he stared at the writing and numbers, he felt Roxanne come and stand beside him, though she said nothing. A quick glance at his team showed them opening binders and books and looking through the contents. He'd get a debrief later. Abandoning the ledger book, he opened the middle drawer on the right and found empty envelopes of various sizes, but organized neatly in the drawer.

The bottom drawer was slightly deeper than the other two and held files suspended on metal sliders attached to the inside of the drawer. File folders were organized alphabetically and were labeled, Derren Bowman, Sylvia Bowman, Leland's parents, Kay Bowman, Brendan Bowman, Matthew Bowman and Roxanne Bowman. His fingers itched to read through that one. But he'd get to it later.

Closing that drawer and moving to the top left drawer he opened it and found it very shallow and empty. Running his hands along the empty drawer he felt for a handle, hole or lock. Gently pushing on the bottom, he listened for any sign the latch would open. Then toward the back of the drawer he felt an indentation in the right side and pushed into it. A click sounded and the bottom of the drawer lifted. Sneaking his finger under the raised board he pulled it open only to realize it was on hinges at the back. Lifting it completely his eyes landed on a thin MacBook laying in the bottom of the drawer.

He heard Roxanne's exhale as she watched him lift her father's computer from the drawer. A glance at her showed him her nervousness. Her mouth was clamped together, and her eyes locked on the laptop. Her right hand rested on her stomach as if to quell the roiling.

"I suppose you have no idea of the password?"

She shook her head slowly, never taking her eyes from the laptop.

Lightly clearing her throat, she responded. "No."

"Okay."

Opening the lid, he watched as the computer came to life. The home screen loaded, and Roxanne's quick intake of breath had his heart racing. If his team wasn't here, he'd pull her into his arms and hold her. As it was, he simply asked "Are you okay?"

She swallowed and blinked rapidly to rid her eyes of the tears that had sprung up. "Yeah."

Looking back to the laptop and the picture of Roxanne and Leland looking at each other and laughing at something upstairs in the kitchen, he could see the love between them.

Pulling his phone from his back pocket he scrolled until he found Gaige's number and tapped his picture.

"What do you have?" Gaige answered.

"We found Leland's laptop. Need you to hack in and see what we have."

"Okay. Grab the Workman and plug it into that."

Wyatt hustled out of the room and within a minute or two came back with a rugged yellow case, with gray rubber on all sides and corners to protect it, the size of a small briefcase. He set it on the desk and opened the lid exposing the micro-server they called the Workman. Inside the lid were holders supporting various wires and adapters. Hawk quickly pulled the appropriate Mac cord from the lid and plugged it into the laptop and the other end into the Workman. Turning the Workman on, he watched as it lit up and began whirring.

Gaige patiently waited on the other end of the line. It wasn't long before he said, "I've got it. Running it through the password bypass now. While we wait, what else have you found?"

"Leland's second office. A room in the basement filled with books and binders. The desk is clean and orderly, everything in its place. We snapped pictures of the binders and books and everything in the drawers. Someone this meticulous must have a precise order and I wanted everything recorded in case we need to recreate."

"Perfect. I knew I had the right man to lead the distance team."

His pride swelled that Roxanne heard that. He'd never much cared before about leading a team or being praised. But he had to admit his heartbeat increased just knowing she'd heard that. "Thanks. A great team helps, and I couldn't do it without them."

"Roger that."

Glancing up at his team he saw them grin, they appreciated the praise, too.

"Okay, I'm in. It'll take a while for me to download and go through the documents. I'll look for anything with those codes on them first. Have you all finished uploading your findings from the emails, texts and GPS?"

Checking silently with his team he watched as they each nodded that they'd completed their jobs. "Ten-four."

"Okay. I'll call you when we've gotten any information. What do you have on the person who was in the safe room and Raymond?"

"That will be our next task." Hawk responded. "We've got

some older pictures from a family album and will run them through facial recognition and see if we can find some local haunts where he might be or anyone who knows him. Maybe his neighbors. We've also uploaded the codes we found."

"Okay. Out."

The line clicked and silence greeted him. He turned to see Roxanne staring at him, a look of awe on her face.

22

"Holy crap you guys have some amazing equipment. Now I really want to know who you are and who you work for."

Axel spoke first. "Ah, we're going upstairs to...do something else."

He shot out of the room with his teammates on his heels without another word leaving her alone with Hawk.

Standing back Hawk turned to look at her and the instant those green eyes met hers, butterflies took flight in her tummy. Laying her left hand over her tummy hoping it would halt their flight, she swallowed the gigantic lump in her throat.

This man before her was turning her head a thousand ways. She'd never met anyone like him. Strong. Powerful. Smart. Fearless. Confident. Virile. Sexy. He had that in spades. Having children was something she'd long ago dismissed as never happening for her, but for God's sake, her womb screamed at her now.

Shaking those thoughts from her head she stepped

back, but his hand reached out and grabbed her hand. The strength and warmth of his hand holding hers sent shivers running through her body. The intensity of his stare damned near made her knees buckle.

"Roxanne."

That's all he said. Her name. And her foolish body responded instantly. She grew wet between her legs and her nipples puckered to the point they ached. Just as she found herself able to say something intelligent, he smiled at her. Fucking. Fantastic. His full lips parted in the most beautiful smile she'd ever seen. Even in a magazine. Especially now, holding her hand and looking at her like he cared.

"Tell me about your tattoos."

He chuckled. "There's time for that later. Each one means something to me. Some missions leave a mark on your soul, some leave tattoos that need to be shared."

"That's beautiful in a sad way."

He shrugged and she could see he was uncomfortable talking about it. "Part of the job."

She swallowed, and for some danged reason, her eyes welled with tears. "Are you always in danger?"

He smiled again and tugged her closer to him. "I'm not in danger now, am I?"

She stood in front of him, the front of her legs bumped up against his knees. His heat circled around her, his scent, his very presence and she tried to remind herself not to get lost in this man. She didn't really even know who he was. All she knew was he and his team saved her, were helping find the killers of her parents and that she was dangerously attracted to him.

"Why did you tear up when you saw that picture of you and your dad on his home screen?"

She took a deep breath to stave off the tears once again. "We were having such a fun day. We were teasing my mom and Brendan took that picture of us laughing." Clearing her throat, she added, "I miss them. Every second of every day."

Hawk pulled her closer still. She craned her neck to look up at him. She was tall for a woman, but he was much, much taller.

"You're probably sick of people telling you this, but it does get easier to deal with. You'll always miss them, but time has a way of easing the extreme suffering and leaving you with the memories.."

"How do you know? Have you lost your parents?"

"Yes and someone who I loved with my whole heart."

Ouch. Why did that hurt to hear? The sadness that washed over his face nearly broke her heart. She released his hand and raised both hands up to wrap around his shoulders. Pressing her body to his she could feel his heartbeat thundering against her shoulder. Strong. Solid. Sexy.

When his arms encircled her body and pulled her closer still the feeling was indescribable. Without thought she turned her face into his neck and kissed along his jaw as far as she could reach. He turned his head and captured her mouth with his and her heart soared. Eagerly she matched his kiss with her own, tasting his lips, exploring his mouth with her tongue, then allowing him to do the same with her mouth. His strong tongue slid along hers in a mating dance, in, swirl around, out, repeat.

One of his hands held the back of her head firmly in place and she rose up on her toes to enable her to reach him easier. He pulled her black t-shirt from the waist of her jeans and one of his calloused hands slid across her back, the friction from his work-roughened hands sent lightning bolts through her body.

Her hands lowered and tugged at his shirt, pulling it from his jeans, her hands eager to roam the satiny skin taut over firm muscles. He was incredible.

She managed to say, "Safe room."

He picked her up and her leg instantly wrapped around his waist as he carried her down the hall and across the basement sitting area to the safe room. He stopped in front of the door, to allow her to enter the password, but his lips kissed along her jaw and down her neck making coherent thought almost impossible.

She fumbled the first time and didn't get the password correct, tried again and was relieved when the door hissed open. He navigated the two steps down into the room, pushed the door closed with his backside and walked her past the unmade bed to the second double bunk bed. Carefully laying her on the bed, he came with her, laying on top of her while not putting his full weight on her.

Pulling at his shirt, she managed to help him get first one arm out then the second allowing her to pull the shirt over his head. Glancing down at his body, her hands again appreciated his body. He reared back, and began pulling at her t-shirt, managing to pull it off easily. She arched up as his hand sought her bra strap and easily unfastened it, then braced himself and tugged her bra away from her and tossed it onto the floor where their shirts now lay.

She watched his eyes roam to her breasts, then his free hand captured a nipple and pinched it causing her to buck under him. He moaned approval then covered her breast with his mouth and sucked it in firmly. She bucked again seeking the friction she needed.

Her hands grabbed at his torso, trying to pull him on top of her but he chuckled and held himself away. "This can't be too quick, Luna, I want to savor you."

She froze at his words and watched his face and his eyes explored hers. "It suits you. It's perfect for you."

He kissed her then so thoroughly she lost all thought but of him. Soon, his fingers found the button and zipper of her jeans and made short work of undoing them. Rearing back on his knees, he tugged at her jeans, but his eyes bored into hers. Her nipples were like pins and goose flesh rose on her body. Her jeans dropped to the floor and he didn't hesitate to strip her of her pink lace panties.

Once those were tossed to the floor, his eyes roamed her body. She felt as if he were caressing her, touching her everywhere. Slowly his hands began working his own button and zipper. Stepping off the bed, he shed his jeans and underwear in seconds. He was magnificent. Muscular and strong, and impressive. In every way.

He climbed over her body, brushing her sensitive skin with his body just barely. It added to the moment and made her want to grab him and pull him down on her with force. But, she also enjoyed watching how he seduced her. It was an interesting mating dance, taking his time, yet touching lightly here and there to see how she responded.

His thick rigid cock rested on her lower belly, just above where she wanted it as he held himself slightly above her. Raising herself up to push into him she saw the grin spread his lips. He'd been waiting for her acceptance.

"Slow and easy or hard and fast?" He husked out between kisses on her neck.

"Both." She managed as her hands sought his back and explored his body.

He chuckled in her ear. "You don't ask for much."

Her tongue rimmed his ear then she nipped his earlobe lightly before whispering. "I want it all."

His response was a groan and that was the sexiest sound she'd ever heard.

His fingers sought her entrance and he slowly worked his fingers in and out of her. She spread her legs wider, allowing him access, her breathing now in short pants, the sounds of his fingers working her mingled with her juices and her moans worked her up to a near frenzy.

Two fingers inside and his thumb found her clit and she damned near lost it. Adding pressure to her clit as his thumb circled, her body convulsed as her orgasm slammed into her. Her vision blurred for a moment and when she came back to earth, she realized she'd bitten his ear lobe.

Kissing the spot she'd just bitten she whispered, "Sorry."

His response was to slide his cock into her, nice and slow. Her swollen tissues accepted him but since they were still so sensitive the feeling nearly sent her right back to orbit.

Slowly he moved himself in and out of her, the steady rhythm keeping her on edge and ready to soar once again. His voice was gruff when he asked, "Tell me when your about ready for hard and fast, Luna."

Oh. My. God. "Now." Her voice didn't sound like hers. And he didn't hesitate.

His pace increased and she got what she asked for. He drove into her at a pace much faster than her heartbeat and firm enough she could feel herself sliding up the bed. It felt fantastic.

Her traitorous body exploded as all of her nerve endings throbbed and ignited. His ragged breathing was the only thing she heard and as his orgasm hit him, he groaned long and loud into the pillow and next to her ear. Best. Sound. Ever.

23

Dazed. Confused. And a bit worried, that he'd crossed a line. Roxanne, while not his client, was certainly someone who relied on him to be professional and do his job. Instead, he'd taken advantage of her vulnerable situation and that was unprofessional. Part of the trouble was, he wasn't sorry. There was an attraction between them he couldn't deny. Lying here now, her head tucked into the crook of his arm, her breathing steady and deep, he enjoyed the feel of her lying next to him. The aroma of her hair tickled his nostrils and the heat of her sexy naked body lying alongside his was hard to resist.

Inhaling deeply, he slowly released the air in his lungs and closed his eyes. Her slender leg moved and slid slowly up his leg, resting with her knee alongside his cock, which now began thickening. Shit.

She sighed, her warm breath brushing over his nipples which caused them to pucker.

"I see you're ready for round two." Her soft voice sleepily acknowledged.

He chuckled deep in his chest. "How about you?"

Stretching like a cat, she rolled to face him, her ice blue eyes crisp and impossible to look away from. "I'm ready."

Leaning up she kissed his lips, the feel of hers soft yet commanding. Her tongue slipped into his mouth, exploring the taste of his tongue. A soft moan from her throat entered his mouth and his cock jumped.

Her smooth movements were impressive as she moved over him, never releasing his mouth. Straddling his cock, she rocked forward then back, positioning the hot head of it at her entrance. Nibbling his lips before lifting her head, a soft smile played on her lips, her eyes locked on his as she slowly lowered herself onto his cock.

Air whooshed from his lungs as he watched her ample breasts sway, her slender waist melded down to the fine white-blond curls between her legs that matched her long hair. Those curls now hid his hardness and her heat encased him perfectly, as if her body were made for his. Their sizes compatible and incredibly paired. It almost made him dizzy.

Then she began the mating dance, rising and falling on him, the brief cool air hitting his cock before her heat enveloped him once more sent chills running up his body. Sensory overload, that's what he had. His eyes feasted on the beauty before him. His body encased in her tight, warm pussy, was something he'd never remembered feeling. Their breathing created a song of lust, their mingled smells filled the air with erotic odors that when blended with all of the above, was like heaven on earth. His hands found her waist and helped her move on him, faster, then back and forth. He watched her mouth form an "o" as her sensitive bud dragged along his cock and his nostrils flared. He wanted to see that again. Helping her move, up and down, up and down, then back and forth he was rewarded with the desire on her face and, as if it were possible, his cock grew harder. His balls rose up and he knew he needed to get her off soon, or he'd beat her there. Repeating his previous ministrations his eyes locked on her mouth as her eyes locked on his. Then she took off. Faster and faster she went, his hands tried slowing her but it was too late. The white-hot pleasure/pain shot up through his cock as he raised his hips, his legs stiffening out behind her ass. She rocked back and forth on him a few times then she cried out her orgasm before dropping down on top of his chest. Both of them breathing heavy from their exertion and trying to even their breathing.

Long moments later she giggled into his chest. "Fucking hot, Hawk. Damn, it's like we're perfectly fitted or something."

His arms wrapped around her body, his fingers tangled into her hair as he thought about her words, knowing he'd just thought them himself. "Yeah." It was all he could say.

He felt himself soften and enjoyed the feeling of his penis slowly slipping from her body and that's when it hit him. They didn't use a condom.

"Roxanne. Shit, we aren't protected."

Her head jerked up and she quickly rolled away. Reaching behind them, she pulled some tissues from a box on the nightstand, handed him one and cleaned herself up with the other.

"Shit." She whispered. "Shit." Again, this time louder.

Her head flopped onto the pillow and she stared straight ahead.

Massive fuck up is what this was. "I'm sorry, I should have..."

"Sorry that we had sex or sorry we aren't protected? You better clarify before I freak the fuck out."

Raising up on his elbow to look into her eyes he said, "Sorry we aren't protected. Not sorry about the sex. You felt fucking amazing."

Her face softened, her hand cupped his face and her thumb brushed over his cheek. "So, did you."

He saw her swallow and he felt sorry for her. Brushing his lips against hers he whispered, "One day at a time."

"Yeah." She inhaled and slowly exhaled. "We'd better get going, the others will be wondering what we're doing."

Twisting, he tossed his legs over the side of the bed and began grabbing their clothing from the floor. Laying hers on the bed, he began putting his on, his mind racing on this faux pas and what they'd do if she ended up pregnant. He'd deal with it like a man if that's what happened and he'd be a father, too. Though maybe one who was away a lot on missions, but it was quality time not quantity, right?

Roxanne gathered her clothes and walked to the bathroom, her naked ass a sight to behold. Pulling his shoes on he listened to sounds and admired the fact that this room was incredibly soundproof. If anyone had to be locked up in here, assailants on the outside would never hear them.

The toilet flushed, the water faucet turned on then off and soon the door opened and a very composed, beautiful Roxanne appeared. Her long white-blond hair swirled over her shoulders, the light from behind her created a halo around her head and he realized the nickname Luna never suited anyone better.

"You're a beautiful woman, Luna."

She froze as she watched him, her perfect teeth biting her bottom lip she cocked her head to the left slightly.

He asked, "Why does it make you pause when I call you Luna?"

"Only family ever call me that. My Grandpa gave me the name."

"Why did he start calling you Luna?"

Tucking her fingers in her front pockets, she relaxed a bit. "We were sitting outside in the dark one night after most of the neighborhood had gone to bed. My brothers, parents and grandma. The moon was nearly full and grandpa looked over at me and said, "Your hair is the same color as the moon. But, you're so similar in many other ways. You're a bright spot in the darkness with your kind ways. You're smart like the moon, keeping yourself at a bit of a distance so you don't get sucked into the gravitational pull that might destroy you. But, you're so pretty to look at. Luna. That would have been a better name for you." She smiled. "I remember those words as if he'd just spoken them this morning."

He stood and closed the distance between them. "I have to say I agree with all of that."

He wrapped his arms around her and pulled her tightly to his body, wanting just a few more minutes of her warmth. When her arms circled him, his heartbeat kicked up and he blew out a breath to keep his control reigned in.

"Ready?"

She nodded against his chest. He kissed the top of her head and turned them to the door. She began entering the code then stopped. "I should make the bed."

He stopped her. Walked to the bed and pulled the covers up. "I'll bunk down here tonight so no one else has to deal with this."

Once he'd walked back to her, she had the code punched in and the door opened. Her eyes glanced at Leland's office and she walked to the doorway. Leaning against the door frame she looked at the wall of binders then gasped.

"Oh my God, Hawk, those acronyms are the same as some of those codes we found. Look, tcl, tic, tm. It's the same."

His eyes scanned the wall of binders and he now saw what she saw. "You're a smart one, Luna." He pulled a binder from the shelf with the letters tic V2.25. "What about the numbers?"

"I don't know."

"Okay, let's go see what's going on upstairs and look at those code sheets again. We'll tell them your theory and see if anyone else has any other ideas."

24

She felt like a teenager again and it was annoying. On one hand, she was giddy that she and Hawk had connected in the most amazing way. It happened so fast and in some ways that made it hotter. But, then she hadn't taken steps to protect herself and that was a thousand percent stupid. She honestly hadn't been interested in anyone in so long that she sort of allowed herself to be swept off her feet. Note to self - use your head.

Opening her laptop, she propped her back against the headboard of her bed. The rest of the house had quieted now that everyone had gone to sleep, so she set her sights on figuring out that code. After all, she was smart and research was one of her strengths, it was about time she used it. These past two weeks she'd wallowed in her grief and despair and sat around waiting for other people to solve this despicable crime. Three people, two who meant the world to her, had been murdered and someone was going to answer for it.

Her thoughts strayed to the basement, more accurately the safe room, where Hawk now slept, without her. He'd insisted that he bunk down there, telling the others that if the person who had been in that room came back, he'd be there to surprise the shit out of him, be it Raymond or otherwise. She knew that was only partly true. Wyatt and Axel took her brothers' rooms and she was grateful to have someone up here in case more intruders decided to visit. Jax and Dodge were in her parents' room, and to her surprise, she only had a slight twinge when she handed out the room assignments and it made the most sense for them to be in there. It would be silly to leave that gorgeous room empty because of who used to sleep in it. And, let's face it, they'd never sleep in there again. Life moved on. She was moving on without them. Though she felt guilty for thinking that, it was nonetheless true.

Typing the first code into her computer, tcl, she watched her screen populate television brands, television companies and more of the same in different languages. Doubting this code had anything to do with televisions or television companies, she thought a bit deeper about this strange acronym and wondered what else it could mean. Typing in tcl - code, excitement skittered around her tummy when the words, "dynamic programming language" populated her screen. Clicking through each of the searches found her mind begin to race through the different ways programing is used. To her knowledge, her father didn't create code for websites or any type of online systems. State Department personnel or the trained military members performed that task. But this did make her wonder if someone her father associated with on base or in the Department had for some strange reason, created a code for a project. This was one avenue to search.

Since Hawk's person, whoever this person was, had finished with her father's computer, it warranted a search on her own of just what was on it. She'd sneak downstairs and grab his laptop and bring it up here so she could further examine what it was she hoped to find. Which was still a mystery, but it was a start.

Closing her laptop lid she scooted to the edge of her bed. Snagging her computer, she quietly padded to the door and opened it a fraction to peek out. Silly, actually, it was her house, but she wanted to be quiet. Having this group of people was nice in that she felt save, but holy hell there was a lot of commotion going on with all of them here. She realized how much she liked her solitude.

No one out and about in the hall, so she slipped from her room, pulled the door closed quietly and made her way down the staircase. From the top of the stairs she looked into the foyer and once again felt the pride she'd always felt for this home. Not many folks had a home passed from generation to generation and she was grateful for this one. So many memories lingered here, most of them good, if you didn't count the events of earlier this morning. Or, actually, since it was now one o'clock a.m., yesterday.

Nearing the bottom step, she averted her eyes from the office and the living room. Still too much to handle at this point. This also led to questions of Azerbaitani and whether the law enforcement agencies were right in assuming the Prime Minister had been the target. Except for the fact that those two men who broke into the house yesterday had also been from Azerbaitani, but why in the hell were they here?

Turning to walk under the staircase and go to the basement through the dining room and kitchen she easily set her laptop on the dining room table. Turning right to the basement door she slowly opened it, grateful it didn't squeak. Slowly making her way down the steps, using her phone flashlight to guide her, she turned left again at the bottom of the steps. Her father's office door was open but before stepping in, she turned to look at the door to the safe room. Shaking her head no and reminding herself to behave and not act like a silly teenager, she stepped into her father's office. Inhaling deeply, she could still smell his aftershave. He'd always worn Old Spice. Oh, how she loved that smell.

Closing her eyes and remembering his smile when he first saw her every time she came home caused her throat to tighten and her eyes misted up behind her closed lids. His hugs were the best, too. His strong arms wrapped around her and held her close as he whispered in her ear, "Baby girl, it feels like forever since my eyes have absorbed your brightness."

Sniffing as her nose began to run, she shook her head and opened her eyes to look at the books with the acronyms on them.

Finding the book with tcl-V2.25 she pulled it from its place on the shelf and hugged it to her body hoping to absorb some of her father's energy. He just couldn't have been involved in anything bad or illegal. She'd never get herself to believe it. Never.

Turning she walked to the desk and sat stiffly in the chair her father had so often occupied. When she and her brothers were little, she understood the need for this quiet office space down here, but why keep it? In some ways she supposed it was like his man cave - military officer style turned State Department Chief of Protocol style.

His computer lid was still up and the screen saver

flashed prisms of color back and forth on the screen. Moving the mouse she waited as the screen saver blipped out then the desktop came into view. Few icons on his desktop, which was her father's style. Not sure where to begin, she clicked on the finder window and typed in the search bar tcl.

The little circle appeared on the screen and then slowly the finder window populated several documents, programs, etc. that contained these three letters together. Once it had completed its search, she shook her head at the long list that had populated. Taking a deep breath, she clicked on the first document and saw more of the same code as the sheets in the safe room. Closing this out, she looked at the next and then the next only to reveal the same thing. What did all of this mean?

Hearing footsteps on the floor above her she froze. Someone was walking around up there. Carefully closing the lid on her father's computer, she listened as the person upstairs turned the water on, then off. The footsteps walked across the floor then a cupboard opened and closed. It took a few moments for her fear to subside and her mind to realize that it wasn't an intruder upstairs but one of Hawk's group. She'd been okay at first, knowing that Wade had sent them in to help. But now she wanted to know how they had all of these resources and who was paying them and why they were here. But mostly, she wanted to know if Hawk always slept with the women he helped out. She was likely just another scared woman in mourning or danger that he slept with then moved on. If that was the case, she'd make sure they didn't sleep together again, and she'd steer clear of him so she didn't get her heart broken. She was dealing with enough as it was, without adding heartbreak to the pile of shit she was managing.

Standing, she picked up her father's laptop and hugged it to her body. Making her way to the door, she stopped and lay the laptop on top of the book on the desk, then picked them both up and softly walked across the basement floor to the steps leading to the kitchen. Whoever was up there was a far cry safer for her to chat with than sitting in the room across from where Hawk now slept. At the top step she looked around the door to see Jax standing with her hands on her hips, her right foot tapping out a quick soft beat, her impatience was clear. Standing in front of the coffee pot, the fresh brewed aroma floated over to her, Jax was irritated at the pace of the coffee maker.

"It'll go faster if you aren't watching it."

Jax turned her head, surprised to see her standing in the doorway. Her lips spread to a saucy smile as she said, "Go down for round two?"

"What?"

Jax giggled, "I think you get my drift."

She could feel her cheeks burn and knew with her light coloring they were flame red.

Jax laughed a strong belly laugh. "You're face just gave it away, Roxanne."

Stepping fully into the kitchen, she took a deep breath and let it out slowly. Deciding to change the subject, because, honestly, she didn't go down for round two. Actually three, but she didn't, so...

"I went down to get my father's laptop. I can't get the code out of my head and wanted to do some searching on his laptop."

Pouring a cup of coffee Jax replied. "That's why I'm up

now. Hawk mentioned your idea about the code, and it was nagging at me, too. Want to work together on it?"

Surprised that Jax would be agreeable to work with her she nodded. Jax held up the coffee pot and raised her eyebrows and Roxanne nodded. Turning to her right and setting her Dad's laptop and book on the dining room table, she came back to retrieve her coffee and add some creamer to it. This could be interesting.

25

Hawk woke with a start. Sitting abruptly, he looked around the room. His breathing was still heavy, and he felt the sick feeling in his stomach every time he remembered the day Sarah was killed. She died in his arms, the sounds of her struggling to breathe still imprinted on his brain. The smell of her blood as it seeped from her body and the look in her eyes as she realized she was going to die. At first, she'd been scared, even though he tried to reassure her. Then, as if she just knew, the look of fear washed away, and a sense of calm fell over her beautiful face. Her blue eyes stared into his as her lips trembled into a smile. Her last word was, "Okay." It came out as only a whisper, but he heard it and knew she meant it was okay, she wasn't scared any more.

The nausea once again crept up his stomach, his head pounded with the beat of his heart. She wasn't supposed to be there. He'd gone after the men who killed his best friend, Colt. He'd tracked them to an old gas station out of town with every intention of killing them so they wouldn't kill anyone else. He'd shot at the first one, wounding him in the leg, then he heard her scream, "No."

He looked over as she ran toward him, yelling, "No, Hawk, don't do this."

Two shots rang out and they shot her. She fell in front of him and in his rage, he leveled his gun on the shooter first and killed him. The wounded man tried to run, but he shot him three times, downing him before he ran to Sarah and held her in his arms. It was Gaige's father, Donovan, who saved him from a long jail term. Self-defense and justifiable homicide were the words he'd used to help Hawk. Sarah had called Van before she got to him. She'd told Van she was afraid he'd kill these guys and sit in prison or worse. Van had gotten there before the police. Van'd taken care of dealing with them while he sat like a stone remembering Sarah's eyes as the life left them. He'd sat empty of emotion, with Sarah gone, during the police interrogation. He'd been numb through all of it. Answering questions as Van had instructed him, he'd managed to stay out of prison. It was fortunate for him that those two assholes were wanted for murder and sadly, it was also fortunate for him that they'd killed Sarah. At least that's what one of the cops had said and it took everything in him not to kill that smart ass. Nothing about Sarah's death was fortunate.

Running his hands over his face and through his hair he worked to shake the sickening feeling that fell over him now. He hadn't dreamed about Sarah's death in months. Why now?

Twisting and setting his bare feet on the floor, he snagged his jeans off the foot of the bed and slipped them on. Not bothering with shoes or socks he stood and grabbed a black t-shirt shirt out of his duffel. Pulling it over his head, he opened the door to the safe room and stepped into the sitting area in the basement of the Bowman home. A quick glance into Leland's office and he noticed the laptop was no longer on the desk.

Turning to the steps he ascended them using his fingers to push his hair away from his face while mentally wiping the nightmare from his mind. He needed coffee. Grabbing his phone from his back pocket, he saw the time was close to three in the morning.

The smell of coffee hit his nostrils at the top of the steps and the soft murmurings of Jax and Roxanne hit his ears. Warning bells went off at what they must be discussing. He'd slept with Jax once, years ago, and for some reason the almost panic he felt that she may have said something to Roxanne nearly made him dizzy.

Rounding the corner to the dining room a set of gorgeous light blue eyes landed on him, slid down his body and back up again in the most sensual suggestive way. His cock twitched as he remembered how he felt sliding into her just hours before. He swallowed and chanced a look at Jax, who grinned then looked at her computer again. She knew. They'd talked. His stomach rolled.

Roxanne finally spoke, "You're up early."

"So are you two."

"Never really went to bed. I couldn't get this code out of my head."

Looking at Jax again he waited for her to say something. Finally she said, "Me too."

One look at the table showed him coffee cups, an opened binder and three laptops splayed across the top. They'd been at this for some time.

"I'm getting coffee, anyone need a refill?" He asked

absently. His mind tried to take in what was happening and how to handle things if Roxanne was pissed or hurt. Why should she be? It was four years ago and Jax was going to marry Dodge and they hadn't even so much as hinted at another tryst after their first one, they both had agreed it had been a mistake and one they didn't intend to repeat. Still, his stomach clenched. Probably from the nightmare.

"I'll take a refill. "Roxanne said, holding her cup up.

He took the two steps toward her and took her cup from her slender hand, though her eyes didn't really meet his. She was pissed.

Slowly walking to the kitchen he wondered what in the fuck had happened to his life from around ten o'clock last night till now? It was as if some dark force crept in and shattered everything. The peace he'd made with losing Sarah, to the things he'd done for GHOST since then to today.

Pouring coffee into Roxanne's cup, he noticed that she liked cream. He'd learned to drink his coffee black from all his time in the field. Pulling the creamer from the refrigerator, he poured a bit into her cup, replaced it in the inside shelf and turned to pour his own coffee. Cups had been set out for them; he didn't know if that was Roxanne or Carmella had done it before she left. It was nice whoever had done it.

Taking a deep breath, he grabbed both cups and made his way to the dining room where silence had fallen.

"I think I've figured it out." Roxanne exclaimed.

Jax stopped what she was doing and looked over at Roxanne.

Roxanne pulled the binder toward them, in between them, then pointed to a spot in the binder, then one on her father's laptop. "It's code written into the games. We need someone who knows how to play to tell us what it means. Or to find the code writer."

He walked to stand behind her and glanced at the laptop and the binder. Setting her coffee on the table he looked closer. Leland's laptop was opened and the home screen of a game was displayed on it. Bright colors and mystical creatures were depicted.

"You found this game on Leland's laptop?"

"Yes, they were hidden but we figured it out and managed to find the hidden files he'd kept them in. There are a lot of games."

His eyes floated from the screen to the binder trying to catch up to her. "Tell me what you think."

"The binders in the basement are affiliated with different versions of codes in games. I don't know what all of the code means, I don't read code, but basically, such as this game, see this." She pointed to small print at the bottom of the home screen. V2.25. "This is the version of a game this code relates too. It seems to be successive, in that we found V2.26 and V2.27. Same with this other code, FO4-3." She clicked a tab on Leland's computer and another game home screen populated. Scrolling to the bottom of the page she said, "Right here." Her slender finger pointed.

"I'll be damned." He whispered.

"So, Leland was playing games?"

"I'll never believe that, Hawk. It wasn't him. He never wasted a minute of any day. Never. I think he was using these games for another purpose. Think about it, if someone can write code into a game, could it also be that someone playing the game would be able to decipher the code for a purpose?"

"I don't see why not."

Jax spoke up then and pointed to another section in the binder they'd highlighted. "We think this is the time frame in the game where the code is found."

He glanced at where she pointed. 18:34. "Could be 18 minutes 34 seconds into the game."

"Yes, that's what we think." Jax responded.

Feeling more positive than he had in a bit, he pulled his phone from his pocket and tapped Gaige's picture.

26

Finally, she felt like she was getting her mojo back. She wasn't sitting on the sidelines letting others work on her behalf. She dug in and in the process she found out a few things. Jax was pretty great. She wasn't a warm fuzzy, but she was smart, efficient and complimentary of Roxanne's efforts. Dare she say, they formed a bit of a friendship? Perhaps. But, what was more important was that they were a bit closer to finding the killer of her parents.

She felt strong. Alive. On top of her game again. Wow, what in the world had happened to her these past few weeks? Note to self - don't shrink into yourself.

The look on Hawk's face when she and Jax showed him what they'd figured out was wonderful. He was happy. They had a good lead. But, thinking of him now, her resolve was waning. What was it about a man wearing jeans and no shoes or socks? His bare feet, finger combed hair, fresh from bed look made her wet. She tried hard not to show it, but damn it, he was a sexy ass man. You'd have to be dead not to notice. But, she didn't want to fall for him, so she averted her eyes and stared at her computer screen to keep from jumping on him. Well, she wouldn't do that, she had more composure than that. At least a little bit. Right? Sure, she did.

Sitting here now, sipping at her coffee she listened as he related everything they'd told him to someone on the phone. Jax dismissed herself to get a few winks she'd said, and Roxanne should have done the same, but she was alone with Hawk and for some strange reason, she sat here as if he were a wizard who'd placed a magic spell on her.

That thought startled her because she remembered something she wanted to check on. A niggly thought in the back of her mind that she didn't have time to check on previously because she and Jax were working through the version issue. What in the hell was it?

"What's wrong?"

Startled by his voice her eyes darted to his. "Ah, nothing. Something. I wanted to remember to research earlier but we were busy and now for the life of me I can't remember what it was but it's bothering me."

"You're probably too tired to think straight right now, go get some sleep and you'll remember in the morning."

"What are you going to do?"

"I'm waiting for Gaige to call back with information on the data we uploaded into the system last night as compared to what you and Jax worked through."

"Who's Gaige to you?"

Watching his chest expand and contract was tantalizing. "He's my boss."

"Boss from where? What company do you work for?"

"Roxanne, you know I can't tell you that."

"Look, I get that you're some super-secret group, but

I'm not stupid. Wade told us to work with you, which means you have military connections. You're all former military, that's clear by the way you carry yourselves and the manner in which you thought nothing of running into danger when I needed help. Wade was best friends with my father. I can keep piecing things together or you could just tell me what's going on."

His back was rigid, and his jaw tight, but when he walked around the table to stand next to her, his sheer size, the fragrance of his aftershave or soap, or whatever swirled around and almost made her dizzy. Then, he kneeled alongside her chair and with one hand, grabbed a chair leg, turned her chair then pulled her close so he was directly in front of her. Those green eyes of his bore into hers and her throat dried. Her heart hammered in her chest and butterflies flipped in her tummy. As if all that wasn't causing her to sway, with his hands, he spread her legs open, rose up on his knees and pulled her chair firmly to his body so she couldn't close her legs. Heat slammed into her cheeks and her chest as the firmness of his body could be felt against her legs.

When he spoke to her, his voice was deep and low. "Stop prying. I'm not at liberty to tell you more."

Then his lips ground against hers, almost uncomfortable at first, but he soon softened his kiss and his hands held her head on both sides as his tongue dipped into her mouth and softly explored. He tasted like fresh coffee and man. His strength was an aphrodisiac and all of her blood and excitement raced between her legs and caused her body to shake at the intensity.

Then, just as abruptly as he had initiated his kiss, he pulled away. He stood and stalked into the kitchen and she was so dizzy she couldn't have followed if she'd wanted to. WTF?

He was maddening.

Wait. That was it. Mad. Mad Max. That was what she wanted to research. A game modification created by a gamer named Backdoor Sorcerer for a game titled Mad Max. She'd seen his name in the binder. Pulling the binder toward her she thumbed through the pages. Grabbing the yellow highlighter, she marked through the places she'd seen his or her name. It was added in footnotes on three pages in the binder labeled GT-4-3.

Looking at the passages marked with the footnote, she saw code, which meant nothing to her, but she decided to add the code to the search engine on her computer and see what popped up.

Her eyes grew as her screen populated with a game name, then a cryptic message. *24 bodies. poison. new site. nov.*

"Someone's passing messages through games." She wasn't really talking to anyone, but Hawk reappeared in the room.

"What?"

"Messages are hidden in the game codes and mods. Look." She pointed to her screen. 24 bodies poisoned. November possibly but I don't know what new site means."

"Where did you come up with this?"

"Here." She pointed to the footnote in the binder.

"Type in the other codes related to footnotes."

She did. Her fingers were shaking and she made mistakes, but easily backtracked and corrected them. The next message was similar. *18 bodies. old site. dec. shooting.*

"Do the next one." His voice was strong and solid and it

helped to calm her and she frantically typed in these messages.

Worse. more dead. complex tainted. help.

Grabbing his phone, he dialed who she assumed was this Gaige, his boss, he'd called earlier.

"We have something big. Was the government in Azerbaitani building a big complex?"

He waited, his eyes scanning the screen of her computer. He stood next to her and his scent floated over her. She was excited with this piece of news and she felt confident they were one step closer.

"No shit? Where?" Hawk sat in the chair alongside her, turned her computer screen and began typing in a new search engine window. A drawing populated the screen of a large government looking building in a remote area, which she assumed was Azerbaitani.

27

"Hawk, we've got intel from Leland's phone. He had been texting someone in Azerbaitani named Zacara Aliyeva. We have several text messages from her to him but they stopped two months ago. Most of them are the code acronym you found and the time stamps Zacara sent to Leland. Leland would send a cryptic message back of similar code. He'd use a different acronym, followed by Backdoor Sorcerer and a time stamp."

"Send me one."

His phone pinged a new text and he promptly forwarded it to Roxanne's email address. Her computer pinged and she opened the email. After reading it she looked at the documents in the binder and scanned through looking for the similar code.

Three pages later she said, "Here." Pointing to the place with the same time stamp, she quickly typed that into a search engine and they read the message together.

Be there in jan. Working on plan. Aligning help now.

Roxanne looked up at him, her eyes glassy with moisture. "My father went to Azerbaitani in January of this year."

She swallowed and his heart hurt for her.

Gaige was still on the line so he snapped out of his stupor named Roxanne, and said, "Can we ping the IP address for these messages? Roxanne is sure Leland didn't know programming, so he was working with someone. We need to know who he was working with to insert this code into these games."

"On it."

"Gaige, we also need help from Casper. What was Leland doing in Azerbaitani this year in January and on his prior visits there? Casper must be able to get the information we need to pull this together."

"I'll contact him and see what he knows. Out."

Setting his phone on the table he turned in his chair, so he was facing Roxanne. She turned to face him and an enormous lump formed in his throat. "Roxanne. What happened yesterday...What I mean to say is, after this mission is over, I have to go back home."

"I know." Her voice was soft and small and belied the strength he knew she had.

"I don't want to hurt you. It's not my intention at all."

She softly cleared her throat. "I know, Hawk."

"It doesn't mean I'm not attracted to you, I think it's clear that I am, but I don't want to mislead you in anyway."

She swallowed and his eyes floated to her neck and the rapid pulse beating just beneath. She took a deep breath and pushed her chair away. "I'm not mislead in any way and I knew from the start you were only here for a while. We both let off some steam and made each other feel good for a few moments. That's it. No promises made." Standing, she closed the lid on her computer, swiped it from the table and began walking around the table toward the staircase. "I'll just get a couple of hours of sleep if you don't mind."

He watched her rigid back as she disappeared around the corner and listened as her soft steps ascended the stairs slowly. Dropping his head, he closed his eyes and tried to get the image of her hurt face out of his mind. It had to be said, but he didn't have to like it.

Standing abruptly, he snagged his phone and coffee cup from the table, deposited the cup into the sink, then made his way to the basement. Putting another floor between them was a good thing.

Entering the safe room, he left the door cracked open, lay his phone on the bedside table and lay his weary body on the bed. Trying to clear his mind of everything he silently wished sleep would come quickly, he felt like he'd been hit by a semi.

"Hawk, she's the one." The sound of ringing drowned out Sarah's voice.

"Sarah? Where are you?"

"I'm not here anymore, she is." More damned ringing.

"Sarah?"

"I'm not here."

Jolting awake for the second time in a day his heart hammered in his chest as the ringing of his phone broke through his sleep fog. Grabbing his phone, he tapped the answer icon and growled, "Yeah."

"I've got the IP address. Guess who Backdoor Sorcerer is? None other than Raymond Bowman."

"No shit?" He dragged his hand through his hair, squeezed his eyes closed to concentrate on Gaige's information and stood hoping to get his blood flowing.

"We'll take a trip over there. Cops should be finished

with their crime scene by now and maybe we can get in and find some clues to his whereabouts."

"Roger that. I'll keep you posted on this data we're crunching here. Great work, Hawk."

"Yeah. Out,"

Tucking his phone into his back pocket, he shook the sleep from his head as he made his way up the stairs. He could hear chatting and knew most of his group was up by now.

As he neared the top steps, he could smell the fresh coffee and his mind perked up a bit. Entering the kitchen Axel and Wyatt were at the coffee pot. Wyatt turned and saw him then held his coffee up as if to wave. "Morning."

"Morning. Get yourselves situated; I've got some intel for you."

"Roger that." Axel mumbled and left the room. He could hear Axel tell the others to get ready for assignments. He had a great team.

Entering the dining room, he noticed all of them there, including Roxanne, who refused to look at him, preferring her laptop over him. Just as well.

"Listen up." He said as he took the chair at the end of the table, his back to the kitchen, and furthest from Roxanne. Sitting too close right now would be difficult.

He began debriefing on all that had transpired through the night. When he mentioned all that Roxanne and Jax had uncovered and then he and Roxanne figuring out the messages in the code, she looked up at him, a soft smile on her face, but nothing more.

"So, I need two of you to go to Raymond's house and see if you can find anything that will tell us where he's at. Gaige just sent me the address of a gamer's home, where apparently gamers can go and sit for hours, or days, playing without being disturbed. They pay for their time like a hotel. Two of you need to check that place out and see if Raymond is there."

He specifically looked at Roxanne. "Roxanne, I need you to text Raymond and ask him to meet with you. I have his number from your father's phone. I suspect he'll know it's you since he's been in constant contact with your family and it appears had helped your father send cryptic messages. We need to talk to him and we need to protect him. I suspect the men or their counterparts, who were here, were the ones who broke into Raymond's house. He is likely a target."

"Okay." Her voice was soft but she looked into his eyes now and he struggled to look away.

Axel then said, "Wyatt and I can go one place. Dodge, Jax, which do you want?"

Dodge spoke first. "We'll take Raymond's house."

"Roger that." Wyatt said as he stood. "We'll be in touch."

Hawk finally looked away from Roxanne to Wyatt and Axel as they moved to leave. "I'm texting you all the addresses. Check in often."

28

S
he knew it wasn't something that would last, but hearing him say it, well that hurt so much more than she dreamed it would. And why? It was dumb. She'd never needed anyone in her life. After a few boyfriends had treated her like a wallet, she'd decided that she was good on her own. She was successful, set for life financially and smart. She had girlfriends, she traveled when and where she wanted and she never felt lonely.

Sitting here looking at Hawk now, her stomach twisted and her heartbeat increased. Maybe she'd been cooped up too long. So, she decided to get out of the house.

"I'd like to go with Jax and Dodge." Turning to look at Jax, she saw a slight grin on the pretty brunette's face, but she said nothing.

Hawk cleared his throat. "Text Raymond first. I'm sending you the number."

She watched his fingers move over his phone screen and within seconds her phone pinged an incoming text.

Opening the text, she tapped on Raymond's phone

number and tapped out a message to him telling him she wanted to see him to talk about her parents' deaths and was he okay? She'd been to his house and saw that something had happened there. Tapping send, she stood and closed the lid on her laptop.

Jax and Dodge did the same and they each grabbed their laptops and headed to the backdoor in the kitchen to walk across the backyard to the drive in the back of the house. No words were spoken by any of them. Climbing into the sleek black SUV her heart felt a bit heavy. She left Hawk alone in the house, but she just couldn't be there with him now. It hurt.

They pulled out of the driveway and headed in the direction of Raymond's house when her phone pinged. Looking at it she saw a response from Raymond.

I'm hiding out. Not safe. Afraid to be seen. Was in the safe room but you have too many people there and I heard gun shots.

Quickly typing back she texted. *Come back to the house. You'll be safe. The people here are good and helping to find the killer(s).*

She read the texts to Jax and Dodge and Dodge pulled the truck over to the side of the street. "If he's on foot, we can pick him up."

Roxanne quickly texted that information to Raymond and they all waited for a response.

How do I know it's safe and this is really Roxanne?

She responded with their family name for Raymond hoping it was the right thing to say to him. *Everything is alright Sonny.*

It seemed like forever sitting and waiting for him to respond. "I wonder if I spooked him." She said it out loud but didn't need a response.

Dodge answered anyway by pulling his phone out and calling someone. "Hawk, Roxanne has made contact with Raymond. Can you ping his phone and get a location?"

Finally after more than ten minutes Raymond responded. *I'll be at the White Dog Black Cat Coffee Shop. I use the backdoor, so when you get there, pull up in the back and wait. I'll come out. What are you driving?*

I'll be in a black SUV, I'll roll down my window in the back so you can see me and know it's safe.

A thumbs up was his response.

Jax quickly typed in the address of the coffee shop on her phone and they took off. Jax turned in her seat and said, "Call Hawk and tell him what we're up to."

Then she smiled a devilish smile and if Roxanne didn't know better, she'd think she was doing this on purpose.

Swallowing as she dialed Hawk's number she took in a deep breath as slowly as she could so it wasn't noticeable. But Jax turned her head and smiled at Dodge and in the mirror, Roxanne saw him grin. Those two were doing this on purpose. But how in the world would they know anything anyway?

His phone rang once and the instant his husky voice sounded over the phone her heart hammered in her chest and her stomach quelled.

"Roxanne, what's going on?"

"Um, we're going to pick up Raymond."

"Where?"

"Cafe. White Dog Black Cat."

"Send me the address and I'll have Wyatt and Axel meet you there in case you need backup."

"Okay."

Before she said something stupid, she ended the call

and relayed what Hawk had said. Her shaking fingers fumbled over the letters and numbers on her phone, but she managed to get the address texted to him. Then she relaxed into the backseat and stared out the window wondering what was wrong with her.

About twenty minutes later they pulled into the back alley of the coffee shop and she rolled her window down. Both Jax and Dodge had their guns out and Dodge never took the truck out of drive in case they had to take off.

"When you see him, don't open the door until he is almost to the truck." Jax told her.

"Okay."

"Then jump out and let him slide in so he's behind me. If he pulls something, I don't want him behind Dodge while he's driving."

"Okay."

The second black SUV containing Axel and Wyatt pulled in behind them. She saw Dodge look in the mirror and Jax turn to look out the back window, then give them a thumbs up.

She felt like a sitting duck with her window down and the other occupants in the SUV on high alert. Then the backdoor opened and she saw him. At least she thought it was him. He looked much older and disheveled from the picture she'd seen of him. How would she really know it was him?

He slowly approached the vehicle, looking side to side and scared for his life. His eyes met hers then looked away quickly and she knew that must be him, he never did make eye contact for long.

As he neared the vehicle, he kept his eyes averted and said, "Everything is alright, Luna."

She looked to Dodge in the mirror, and he nodded once.

Opening the door, she stepped out of the vehicle and motioned for him to get in. Quickly sliding in after him, she closed the door, rolled up the window and set about attaching her seatbelt.

At a loss for what to say, she looked at Raymond, but he continued to stare ahead. "Raymond, this is Dodge and Jax. They are part of the team helping to find the killer or killers of Mom, Dad and the Prime Minister."

Without inflection or emotion Raymond responded. "I already know who them."

Jax turned in her seat and looked at him. When he didn't respond further or look at Jax, her eyes darted to Roxanne's then back to Raymond. "Who killed them killed Raymond and do you have proof?"

Raymond's hands lay perfectly still over each knee. His back was ramrod straight. "The Azerbaitani Prosperity Party."

Dodge glanced into the mirror then back to the road. "Do you have proof?"

"Some. Leland had been compiling data to bring them down. They are killing members of the other parties. Mass genocide. They want control of the government and they've been killing people in large numbers and burying them on the site where the new government building is to be built."

His voice shook slightly but his posture never relaxed.

"How do you know?"

"Leland had had a contact trying to help him. Her mother and brother were killed in one of the poisonings."

"Can we contact her?" Jax was taking notes now.

"She's dead."

Roxanne tentatively reached over and touched his shoulder. "When did she die?" She asked softly.

She saw Raymond swallow, but he never turned his face to her. "Two days before Leland and Kay." He swallowed again and she saw his eyes well. "They were found out."

29

"**F**antastic. Bring him back here to the house and we'll see if we can get more information from him."

Ending the call with a tap of his thumb he set his phone on the dining room table. It was beginning to look like this particular mission was over. Maybe his gut wouldn't hurt so much once he got back home. Hopefully his nightmares would stop, too.

Getting up from his chair he took his empty coffee cup to the sink, rinsed it then set it in the dishwasher. Carmella came in from the front of the house just as he closed the dishwasher door. "Thank you, Mr. Hawk."

He chuckled. "You're welcome, Carmella. Thank you for cooking and cleaning. Roxanne and all the Bowmans are lucky to have you."

"MmHm. I'm lucky, too. They pay me well, treat me with respect and I love my job. Most of my friends can't say the same."

"Then, I'd say you're all lucky. I hope my team and I weren't too much of a burden."

"Naw, you're all good. Weird hours though."

She brushed past him to the refrigerator and pulled a big roast from inside. Setting it on the cutting board on the counter, she pulled a pile of potatoes from the drawer inside the fridge and set them next to the roast.

"I don't want to be rude, Mr. Hawk, but you're in my way now."

He chuckled. "I can take a hint. I'll be downstairs until the others get back if you need me."

He snagged his phone off the dining room table, then turned to go downstairs. It was doubtful they'd be leaving tonight, but he wanted to be ready for whenever they did leave. He'd make a quick exit so it didn't prolong this painful thing between him and Roxanne.

Entering the safe room, he closed the door, then went into the bathroom to take a quick shower. He turned the water on to warm and pulled clean clothes from his go bag. Making quick work of his clothes, he left them in a pile on the floor, eager to clean up. The warm water hit him and a shiver ran the length of his body. It had been a couple of days. Longer than that since he'd had any time alone to actually think. Lathering the shampoo into his hair he closed his eyes and as if it were trying to betray him, his mind went instantly to Roxanne and how she felt yesterday as they made love. Wait, had sex.

Shaking his head to change the direction of his traitorous thoughts he rinsed his hair and grabbed the bar of soap in the dish. Managing to clean up without further sexy thoughts he stepped from the shower and toweled off.

Getting dressed he told himself it would be good to get home. Back to whatever normal was. Maybe looking forward to his next mission. Hopefully that would be in the rainforest, devoid of women. A woman in particular. He needed to get her out of his head.

Just as he leaned over to pull his boots on, he remembered they'd had unprotected sex. He'd need to keep in touch just until he knew she wasn't pregnant. Fuck.

Tucking his phone into his pocket, he wrapped his dirty clothes together and stuffed them in his go bag.

Looking around the room he checked for anything personal he had laying around. It was doubtful, he rarely brought anything personal with him on a mission. He had his phone which had pictures on it of Sarah, and his parents and Colt- all gone now. Other than that, he didn't collect personal things, sometimes they just hurt too much.

Which brought him back to Roxanne. Sighing deeply, he pulled the covers up, tucked in the sheets and made the bed. Turning he washed the couple of glasses used for water in the sink and turned them over to dry. Wiping the small counter down, he then went back into the bathroom to make sure he didn't leave anything in there.

30

"How? Who found them out?" She could hardly control herself. They were getting close to the answers she needed.

Jax reached between the two front seats and laid three fingers on her knee. Her eyes met Jax's and what she saw was compassion and a silent plea to let her handle this. Lifting her phone up Roxanne could see Jax was recording and she reminded herself that this is what these people did for a living.

Swallowing the lump in her throat she nodded once and let Jax handle it. Dodge put the car in gear and they moved through the back street and turned out onto the main road to take them back to the house.

Raymond inhaled deeply and let it out slowly. "I don't know how they were found out. I couldn't contact with Zacara before she was killed."

"How do you know she was killed and didn't have an accident?"

"As soon as Leland and Kay were killed, I tried to make contact with Zacara by the phone number I had for her.

Leland had told me to never call that number unless something bad had happened to him. When I did call it, another person, a woman, answered and said Zacara had been killed three days prior."

"But she didn't say how?"

Raymond glanced her way once then his eyes went to the back of Jax's seat.

"Who are you?" He'd said it softly, but they all heard it.

Jax continued in a soft voice. "We've been hired to find the killers of the Bowmans and the Prime Minister."

"Why?"

"The State Department, the FBI, and the police haven't turned up any leads in two weeks. We have better equipment and less restrictions on how we acquire information."

He breathed in and out slowly for a few seconds. She was no nurse, but she could tell he was scared and trying to figure out if he was safe. He looked her way again. His eyes capturing hers, "Are you sure it's safe?"

"I'm absolutely positive. Two men broke into the house yesterday. The shots you heard were these people stopping them. One of the men then shot himself. They saved Carmella and I."

He swallowed again and looked at the seat back.

Jax looked around the seat again and asked. "Raymond, how long had you been working with Leland on the code and who had you been sending it to?"

His fingers tensed and released on his knees a few times, his back was still ramrod straight. "About a year and a half. Maybe a bit more. He had asked me to write some code for some games for him. I had told him code wasn't really used anymore, gamers now use Mods or modifications. He had said it would be okay, since Azerbaitani was still a little behind the times with some of the entertainment games."

Jax was quiet and Dodge easily turned a corner as they all waited for Raymond. "So, I did. I had written code for three games and then Leland had told me to contact Zaira on Play Station, who had been Zacara, and had sent her the version of the code. When she'd come online, I had just told her V12-3 or whatever the version it had been. Then had said, 18, meaning 18 seconds. That had been the location of the game where she had found my message."

Jax nodded. "What had been your messages? What had Leland been telling Zacara?"

Raymond cleared his throat. "He had been asking for locations where poisonings were occurring. He had been asking for numbers of people killed. How the poison was administered. And, where the bodies were buried."

"And Zacara had then given you the answers?"

He shook his head. "Not right away. The following day I had gotten the code in the same way from her."

"So, those binders in the basement contain all the locations and numbers of people killed by the Azerbaitani Prosperity Party?"

Raymond only nodded.

"Raymond?" Jax waited for him to look at her. "Why are you telling us so much without prompting?"

"They're after me now. I've been found out, too. I'm scared."

Roxanne felt so sorry for him. He had no friends and the only person he had in the family he trusted was dead. She hesitated then reached over and lay her hand over his left hand, still clinging to his knee. His hand was cold and stiff, but she didn't care. He was family, though she didn't really know him well. And he had been helping her father do something good. After long moments, he turned his hand over and locked his fingers with hers, his eyes still staring straight ahead.

She'd take that as a good sign. They sat quietly like that until they reached the house. Once they parked in front of the garage, she opened her door and stepped out. Looking into the vehicle at Raymond she saw him still sitting straight as an arrow and unmoving.

"Hey, it's okay. They'll protect us."

Sucking in a deep breath he released it then slid across the seat to exit from her side of the vehicle. After he stepped out of the truck, she locked her arm in his and walked across the backyard with him, grateful for the tall shrubs that surrounded their house and the semi-privacy. A loud bang rang through the air and Raymond bolted for the backdoor, practically dragging her with him. Jax, Dodge and Axel pulled their weapons and were taking cover at various locations. Wyatt had also pulled his weapon, but he now stood in front of her and Raymond and was walking backward toward the house. "Get inside and go down to the safe room. Hurry." He growled.

She wasted no time and neither did Raymond. They bolted through the backdoor and across the kitchen floor. Carmella was in the kitchen and she yelled. "Safe room now, Carmella."

Carmella followed them down the basement steps, muttering something in Italian, hopefully a prayer. Grateful the door was ajar, they entered the safe room, she turned to close the door after Carmella made her way in and locked it.

"What's going on?" Hawk's deep and still sexy voice called out.

Startled, she turned to see him sitting on the bed. The

one they'd made love in just yesterday. Raymond stood stock still, Carmella went to the sink and washed her hands. That left her to explain.

"We heard a loud bang, like a gunshot as we were walking across the backyard. Wyatt told us to get down here."

Hawk stood and stalked to the door. Pressing the code, he turned as he pulled it open, "Stay here until I give the okay. Listen to me this time."

He disappeared faster than she could respond. Hmm, 'this time', like she was a child or something.

She looked over at Raymond and Carmella and said, "Let's get comfy."

31

S teadily making his way up the stairs, his ears trained on anything that would give him a clue as to what was going on. At the top of the steps he paused, listened and when all he met was silence, he eased himself into the kitchen, keeping his back to a wall. Peering into the dining room he saw it was empty. Inhaling, he turned back to the kitchen and looked through to the living room, which still had no furniture or carpeting. Anything or anyone in that room would cause it to echo throughout the house.

His heart hammered in his chest. Someone was continuing to get too close to Roxanne and/or Raymond. One thing he knew for sure, they'd have to kill him to get to her. He wouldn't watch another woman he cared for die in his arms. That's why he had to finish this mission and leave. His job had cost him his wife a long time ago. He just couldn't go through anything like that again.

He made his way across the kitchen floor and to the backdoor. Wyatt stood to the left of the backdoor and turned his head quickly, nodded then looked back, making a sweep of the surrounding area. Hawk stepped outside and stood to Wyatt's right on the opposite side of the door.

"What do you have?" Hawk asked.

"Not sure yet. No movement after the shot. The others have gone off to investigate the surrounding area."

"Roger." Hawk moved along the wall to the East side of the house and peered around the corner. None of them had their comm units on, so communication was stunted. He saw no movement in the shrubs or hedges, but surveyed along the bottom and at any sparse areas for movement or clothing.

"It's clear out front." Axel said as he rounded the corner.

Hawk nodded. "The others see anything?"

"I don't think so. Dodge is down the street to the East, Jax to the West. Neither has said anything and no shots have sounded."

"Roger. I'll wait out here till they come back."

"Great. I've gotta piss like a racehorse." Axel moved past him and easily ducked into the house.

Dodge whistled, two short one long, which meant all was okay. Soon, Jax returned the whistle signaling the same. Once they all were in the house, they'd secure it tightly and get the cameras and security system turned on.

Waiting for the last two team members he rested his back against the wall and thought about Roxanne. He could tell she was scared, but she wasn't a shrinking violet. As a matter of fact, her voice wasn't even shaking. Tough chick right there.

Dodge whistled again, only he was closer this time.

"All clear." he said loud enough to be heard. Hawk

peered around the corner and saw the tall 6'2" blond man sniggering at him. "I don't want to get shot, buddy."

"I won't shoot you. That's not saying there haven't been times I wanted to."

"Right back 'atcha, big guy."

Dodge walked past him and went to stand close to Wyatt, waiting for Jax to come back. He had to admit, he envied Dodge and Jax. Not that he was jealous. His history with Jax was over years ago. It was what they had together he envied. There once was a time he had that, too.

A whistle sounded and Dodge responded, then walked to the far corner of the house to greet her. A quick peck on the lips and then they all came to stand close to him.

Jax started. "I didn't see anything. But I did hear a car backfire a block over. Could have been that. Maybe it was closer to us when we heard it. But, there isn't anyone lurking that I could see."

Dodge reported as well. "I didn't see anyone, either. Nothing that looks suspicious, no cars out of place on the street."

"Okay. Let's go in and get the alarms and cameras set. I'll get Axel's report, which I assume will be much the same as yours."

Letting out a long breath, relief swam through him but his stomach twisted once again knowing that this mission had gotten personal.

He let the others precede him into the house then he turned and locked the door and set the alarm system. The roast Carmella had put in the oven had filled the kitchen with the most delicious aroma and his stomach growled. Walking to the basement door, he spied Dodge and Jax in his peripheral vision kissing and he swallowed the lump in his throat.

Breathing deeply as he descended the stairs to the basement and closer to Roxanne, he steeled himself to seeing her again.

Entering the code on the door, he opened it and there she was, sitting on the bed he'd made love to her on, looking like a goddess. Her long blond hair flowed over her shoulders, her light blue eyes locked on his and he saw her inhale deeply and swallow. They were getting too wrapped up in each other, it was time to go.

Clearing his throat, he said, "All clear."

"Thank you, Mr. Hawk." Carmella said as she breezed back. "My roast better not be dry."

He chuckled as she passed by him. Looking at the sofa alongside the door he saw a scared man, sitting up straight, his back stiff as a board. His blond hair was in need of a cut; his blue eyes were locked on something straight ahead but didn't appear as if they were seeing anything. His hands lay on top of his knees, his knuckles white.

Roxanne stood and walked to the man, kneeling in front of him. "Raymond, this is Hawk. He's in charge of the group helping us."

Raymond turned his head, briefly looked his way, never quite meeting his eyes, then nodded and resumed his position of staring straight ahead.

Moving his gaze to Roxanne, he said, "Are you alright?"

She stood and moved toward him. "Yes. Just nervous, as you can imagine. That was too many times in just a few days to be comfortable."

His hand reached out and cupped her cheek. His

thumb gently caressed her soft face. She tilted her head into his hand and his heart hammered in his chest.

"Let's he..." He had to clear his throat. "Let's head upstairs and debrief."

He watched her swallow a couple of times, then she stepped back and walked to Raymond. Touching his shoulder, she waited as he eventually stood. Linking her arm with his she began walking to the door, Raymond obediently following along.

Taking a deep breath, he followed them out of the security of the safe room and began their climb to the first level.

32

That confirmed it, Hawk felt something for her, but he was fighting it. Well, she didn't have the time or the patience to try to convince a pig-headed man why he should be embracing their relationship for crying out loud. Not that they had a relationship. What did they have? Nothing really, but it sure did hurt. She had feelings for him. He was the first man in so long that she felt this...what? Connection. That was it, she felt a strong pull to him. Probably some ludicrous protector/victim thing she'd read about.

She walked just in front of Raymond, no longer hanging on to him. He was quiet and had been for some time. She didn't know him well and wasn't sure if that was a natural response for him when he was scared and she had no one to ask, either.

The aroma of Carmella's roast reached her nostrils before she got to the top of the steps. She inhaled and her stomach growled. She hadn't eaten much these past three weeks, not since her parents were murdered. Then, all the commotion at the house had caused her appetite to continue to dwindle. Now, all this with Hawk, well, look how that was turning out.

"Okay, you all go in the dining room and sit down to eat. I'm almost ready to bring it all out." Carmella ordered. She reminded herself to say an extra thank you prayer to God for Carmella tonight, she was certainly a God send.

Waiting for Raymond she looked into his eyes as he reached the top step. "Are you hungry?"

He nodded and her heart hurt for him. "When was the last time you ate a meal Raymond?" She whispered it so she wouldn't embarrass him.

His eyes welled with tears, but he quickly swiped them away. "A couple of days. The cook at the cafe gave me some food, but I wasn't hungry."

She stepped to him and wrapped her arms around his shoulders. She needed to hug him and hoped he needed her hug. When his arms wrapped around her waist and he sniffled, she knew he did. Then her eyes welled with tears. They were a sad pair right here.

A soft pat on her back had her turning to see Carmella. Whispering she said, "Ms. Roxy, please go and eat before it gets cold."

She hugged Carmella then and whispered in her ear. "I love you, Carmella."

Carmella patted her back a few times and whispered back, "I love you, Ms. Roxy."

Taking a deep breath, she straightened her posture, nodded to Raymond and walked with him to the dining room where the others were sitting. Two spots remained at the table at the far end on either side of Hawk. Steeling herself to sit next to him she walked to the side of the table to Hawk's left and motioned for Raymond to sit down. Walking behind Hawk and to the chair on his right, she sat quietly without a word. Placing her napkin on her lap she looked up and saw Jax watching her. Jax winked and grinned and she had to admit, that made her feel better.

Carmella began bringing the food to the table, beginning with the potatoes and huge bowl of cooked carrots. Setting them at the far end of the table, closest to the kitchen, Dodge began digging in without a word. Filling his plate with both vegetables, he then passed the dishes to his right and Jax followed suit.

Hawk leaned into her and softly asked, "Are you alright?"

Her stomach flipped and butterflies immediately swirled around in her belly. Braving a look into the solid green eyes that now entrapped hers, she nodded then replied. "Yes, I'm fine. It's just been a...different sort of week. Actually month. One I hope to never repeat."

The grimace that marred his handsome face made her feel sad, but he steeled himself and sat back just as Carmella brought the roast down to Hawk and handed it to him. "Careful, Mr. Hawk, the plate is hot."

"I got it Carmella. It looks fantastic."

She patted his shoulder then scurried off to the kitchen. Knowing from her years of experience that Carmella ate alone in the kitchen, which used to bother Roxanne to no end; but Carmella told her, "This is my job and I do it to the best of my ability. You are my employer; we don't eat together. Besides, I like my solitude, I don't get much of it any other time and when I go home, I am never alone."

Hawk passed the roast to Roxanne, but she inclined her head to Raymond silently telling Hawk to make sure

Raymond ate first. His lips formed a straight line but he immediately moved the plate to sit in front of Raymond.

Raymond placed a neatly sliced piece of roast on his plate, then Hawk, using his fork, scooped up a piece of the steaming hot aromatic meat and lay it on her plate. "Eat."

She bit the inside of her cheek and her eyes landed on Raymond's who was watching her intently. He nodded his head to her plate and began cutting the meat on his plate.

She could take a hint. Soon the carrots and potatoes made their way to her and she took a small spoonful of each and passed the bowl to Wyatt who sat on the other side of her. Axel completed the circle around the table and the talking stopped as everyone ate as if they hadn't eaten in weeks. Nibbling at her food, she managed to eat more than she'd have guessed she would, but it had been a while since she'd eaten anything to amount to a stomach full.

As their plates began to clear Hawk said loud enough for the whole table to hear, "After we finish, we need to talk to you, Raymond. Anything and everything you can tell us to find the actual killer of Mr. and Mrs. Bowman and the Prime Minister."

Raymond nodded, lay his fork next to his plate and sat back in his chair, his back once again rigid.

33

The living room was still bare so they either had to sit around the dining room table or they could move to the basement sitting room, which Hawk decided was probably the best. Raymond would likely be more comfortable down there; it would seem more casual and less like an interrogation. And the whole team and Roxanne had spent enough time with their asses in the dining room chairs. The Bowman house was posh for sure, but enough was enough.

He looked around the table and noted that everyone had finished eating, the chatter and ball busting had started and Raymond grew more nervous with each second that passed. "Let's grab our laptops and head to the sitting room in the basement. Five minutes."

Without waiting for a response he stood and took his plate to the kitchen where he found Carmella sitting at the kitchen table reading a book and eating her supper. She started to get up when he entered but he shook his head. "Sit, Carmella, we can each bring our plates in here and then we're heading down to the basement, relax a bit."

"Mr. Hawk, I am relaxed."

He grinned at her. Her accent and the use of his name with Mr. in front of it was cute as hell. "Then relax some more."

He winked at her and her cheeks tinted pink. Not as bright as Roxanne's cheeks but it made him feel good that he could make her blush. Stupid thing really, but guys liked it when they could tease a woman and get a bit of a response.

He descended the steps to the basement and immediately counted the number of places to sit. There were five GHOST members and Roxanne and Raymond. The sofa would sit three, two recliners took care of all but two. Pulling Leland's desk chair out to the sitting area and the chair in the safe room, he accommodated all of them.

Grabbing his laptop from his duffle he went back to the sitting area and sat in Leland's desk chair. It was an expensive executive chair with arms and he hoped it sort of made a statement. Leland was the man of the house, the king here. Sitting in his chair would hopefully convey to Raymond that Hawk was in charge and the familiarity of Leland's chair might relax him. It should convey to him why they were all here and might help him remember and relay all the information he had for them.

Light footsteps sounded on the steps and he knew Roxanne was on her way down. Closing his eyes he inhaled deeply, till his lungs burned, then slowly let it out. How was he going to get her out of his head?

"Where would you like us to sit?"

Opening his eyes he saw her shyness and her beauty all at once. She was beguiling. Her long blond hair swept over her shoulders and the contrast with the black long-sleeved sweater she wore accented the lightness of her coloring. Her light blue eyes reminded him of ice, but not in a bad way. There wasn't a sinister bone in her body. Calm, cool, collected and strong as iron.

"Why don't you and Raymond sit on the sofa where it's comfortable and the rest can filter in around in the other seats."

She walked past him to do as he asked, and the aroma of her spicy scent made his heartbeat kick up about ten beats.

Loud footsteps on the stairs brought his mind to the task at hand and he opened his laptop and logged onto the GHOST system.

Jax took the seat next to Roxanne and Raymond on the other side of her filled the sofa. Dodge and Wyatt took the recliners and Axel sat in the armchair he'd brought out from the safe room.

He began. "Raymond, I've listened to what you told Roxanne, Jax and Dodge in the vehicle on the way here but I'd like to ask you a few more questions about Azerbaitani and the political parties there that seem to be at war."

Raymond only nodded, his hands firmly on his knees, his back straight.

"You mentioned you were found out. How do you know you were found out?"

Raymond cleared his throat. I got a text from Leland. It said, "Secure Yourself." That's what he told me he'd text me if he felt we were in danger."

"When was this?"

He watched Jax typing on her computer and knew she'd read that text, looking for the date and time no doubt.

"Two days before he was killed." Raymond responded.

"So, that was the same day Zacara was murdered."

"Yes."

Jax nodded at him and he continued. "Do you think Leland knew Zacara had been killed?"

Raymond's voice shook, "I don't know. He didn't give me any more details."

"What did you do when he texted secure yourself?"

"I was supposed to leave my house with only a few essentials and get out of town."

Hawk's brows drew together. "But you didn't leave town."

Raymond swallowed. "No." His eyes welled with tears and Hawk gave him a minute to compose himself.

"Why didn't you leave town if that was your plan?" Hawk lowered his voice.

Raymond's eyes captured his which was unusual for this man. "I was worried about Leland and Kay. They weren't leaving. I knew Kay was having coffee with a friend, Leland had told me the day prior that Kay always went to the coffee shop on Tuesdays with her friend. I went there to see if she was alright."

Roxanne sat forward and twisted to look at Raymond. "Mom saw you. She thought someone was stalking her that looked like you."

"She couldn't have seen me. I never came out of the building across the street. I left through the backdoor."

"But she was so sure. I remember her telling me she thought someone who looked like you was stalking her."

"I wasn't stalking her. And, I'm positive she never saw me. She sat at the little corner table on the patio and her back was mostly to me. I was in the clothing store across the street and peered through clothing racks just to see if she was okay. She seemed happy and she and her friend laughed and chatted for a long time. I was puzzled about it all. Why would Leland tell me to secure myself but then not secure himself and Kay?"

Roxanne's brows drew together but she sat back into the sofa, confusion on her face.

Hawk continued his questioning. "What was Leland's plan in this case?"

Raymond shrugged. "I'm not sure. I knew the Prime Minister was coming to America and I assumed that he planned on talking to him about some of this, and then he and Kay would leave town for a while. He had better connections for things such as this than I did. I was supposed to go to a second cousin's farm in Oklahoma for a few weeks."

"Okay." Glancing at his computer screen, he looked over the information they'd pieced together thus far. "So, you left the clothing store by way of the backdoor and then what did you do?"

"I went home. I tried to get another message to Zaira, just in case she wasn't really dead. I figured it couldn't hurt."

Hawk nodded his head. "Did you hear anything back from her?"

Raymond slowly shook his head.

"Then what did you do?"

His left shoulder raised and lowered. "I stayed in the basement, hidden. I didn't turn on the lights unless I had to."

"Okay. So, you planned on staying put until you knew Leland and Kay were okay?"

"I knew the Prime Minister was coming, so I hoped that after that visit, Leland would contact me and I'd know how the visit went. I was never sure if the Prime Minister was aware of the information that was passing between us and Zaira. I suspected that he was, but I don't know for sure."

"Okay, then you heard that Leland and Kay had been murdered with the Prime Minister?"

He stifled a sob and his eyes instantly welled with tears. He only nodded.

34

Tears rolled down her cheeks and she swiped them away. A friend had told her there would come a day when she'd be able to remember her parents and smile, not cry. She looked forward to that day. Her father had been trying to do a good thing.

Then, a question popped into her head. "Raymond, why didn't Dad just go to someone in the government who could help him compile this information so he wasn't in so much danger?"

Raymond turned his head to face her, his eyes only flicked to hers once, then he looked at the floor. "He said he'd be shut down and would never get clearance to dig so deep."

Nodding she glanced at Hawk, his sharp green eyes were watching her so intently. She wanted to be immature and stick her tongue out at him or something, but instead she remembered how his arms felt when he held her. They were getting close to leaving and she'd have only her memories to keep her warm at night. She never wanted to forget how he felt when he slid inside of her. How he looked in the throes of passion. How he smelled, the sound of his voice, the whole of him. Somehow in a short amount of time he'd gotten under her skin like no one had before.

"Okay, last question. Do you have any idea who actually shot the Bowmans and the Prime Minister?"

His eyes were on her when he asked the question. She looked into them and saw regret, but she knew he had to ask.

"I don't know. I keep telling myself that TSA or some other agency should be able to pull airline records and find Azerbaitani citizens who've recently traveled here. At a minimum it's a place to start."

"Thanks, Raymond. I assume you'll be staying here tonight, so if we have more questions I'll ask. You'll be safe here, you have my word." Hawk finished and the others closed their laptops and stood to leave.

They nodded at Raymond as they walked past and up the stairs and she felt him relax a bit. Which was the first time he'd relaxed since she'd found him this afternoon. He was likely exhausted.

Hawk was the last member of his team left and he waited to speak until the others were gone. He pushed her father's chair into the office, then stepped out and said, "I'll grab my gear and bunk down with Axel and Wyatt so Raymond can have the safe room to himself."

She was caught off guard at his statement and he brusquely walked to the safe room before she could get her thoughts together. He emerged with his duffle bag tossed over his shoulder and stopped in front of them. "Thanks, Raymond. I know that was difficult and we appreciate it."

Then he disappeared up the stairs. She inhaled and let it out and Raymond softly said, "You love him."

She opened her mouth to speak but nothing came out. Raymond scooted to the edge of the sofa and stood. Walking to the safe room he disappeared through the doorway and she sat like a stone puzzling over his words. Of course, she didn't love him. She barely knew him. For crying out loud, she didn't even know the name of the company he worked for. It was all too secretive and underground.

Standing she walked to the door of the safe room, Raymond sat on one of the made beds against the far wall. "If you want that bed," she nodded to the one she had shared with Hawk, "I can get fresh sheets and make it up."

Raymond shook his head. "No, I'm fine. But, I don't have any clean clothes. Do you think Leland would have something that I could wear? Or one of the boys?"

She hadn't even thought to ask and now she felt like a terrible host. After all Raymond had done for her family. "Of course, let me see what I can find for you. I'll be right back down."

Hoping that Jax and Dodge weren't in her parents' bedroom doing something she didn't want to interrupt, she climbed the steps. Relief swarmed over her when she heard the group upstairs talking about next steps.

Walking from the kitchen into the dining room she looked for Jax. The petite beautiful brunette stood across the room from her and it struck her once again, how different they were and yet so similar in many things. They'd worked well together last night and even had a couple giggles. Clearing her throat, she said to Jax, "Raymond needs clean clothes and I'd like to look through my dad's things for something he can wear. Do you mind?"

Jax's smile was brilliant when she responded. "No, of course not. I'll go with you."

Jax waited for her at the door leading to the front entry hall and then they began walking together. Climbing the steps they were both quiet, the same with the trip down the hall. Jax preceded her and opened the door, letting Roxanne enter the room first.

Entering the room her stomach tightened. She'd purposely not come in here since her parents passed. Looking at it now, memories hit her one at a time like a sledgehammer. Sitting in bed with her parents when she was scared as a little girl. Running in here on Christmas morning eager to open gifts. Birthday's for each of them when she and her brothers tried making breakfast in bed.

Tears rolled down her cheeks as she looked around the room at the subdued colors of blue, gray and white with splashes of burgundy. Jax and Dodge were neat and very little of their things were visible. A warm arm circled her shoulders and her strength was hard to miss.

"I lost my father and my brother within a few years of each other. I know what you're going through and I can tell you, it does get easier to handle, but there will always be little holes where they used to fit in your life."

She simply nodded as she swiped at her tears with the pads of her fingers. Jax stepped to the nightstand and pulled a couple tissues from the box there and brought them to her. "If you want me to look for something for Raymond, I'm happy to do it."

"Thank you. I don't want to be a baby and I've got to go through their things eventually."

Jax swiped at a tear with her thumb and whispered. "I know this has been hard. Made harder by your feelings for Hawk, knowing he'll be leaving soon. I'm sorry."

"I don't have..."

"Shut up. We can all see it. Seriously, the way you two look at each other it's obvious."

Staring into those sharp brown eyes, she had to admit to herself, yes, she had feelings for Hawk. But, she wouldn't beg. Not for him to stay and not for him to take her with him. She had her pride.

35

Getting his head in the game was easy, keeping it there with Roxanne sitting just a chair away, was the problem.

"Okay, Dodge, get on the phone to Gaige and see what either he or Jared can come up with as far as TSA records, or other travel reports on Azerbaitani citizens or any citizen coming and going from there."

Looking at Wyatt, "You and Axel scan through those binders downstairs and see how many bodies we're talking about. Ask Raymond for help if you need it. Catalogue dates and numbers."

Jax stood with her arms crossed over her chest waiting for her orders. "Jax, can you access the reports of the shootings and see if there is any further evidence of where the shots were fired from?"

"Got it."

That left him. And Roxanne.

His eyes met hers and his mind went blank. That's when Jax saved his ass.

"Roxanne, why don't you help me scour through the

law enforcement and DS records for information on the shootings. If you can stand it."

Roxanne stood. "Yes, I want to know as much as I can. Thanks."

The two women walked out of the room and he had this uncomfortable feeling they were growing too close. He was one to talk.

The dining room was now empty, and he decided to go up to Wyatt and Axel's room, where he'd bunk down tonight on a smaller bed in the room which was for one of Roxanne's nephews, and check emails and write more in his report to Gaige.

"Mr. Hawk, can I speak with you?"

Carmella stood in the doorway between the kitchen and dining room, an apprehensive look on her face.

"Of course, what can I help you with?"

She motioned with her hands to the kitchen and turned to walk inside. He followed her to the far corner, where a window overlooked the backyard and the pantry door to its right stood ajar.

With her voice lowered Carmella said, "Mr. Hawk, I need to tell you what I see here and I don't want to get in trouble."

"You won't get in trouble, Carmella."

"But, I don't want Miss Roxy to think I spy on the family members. Don't tell on me, please."

He placed a hand on her shoulder and looked into her worried brown eyes. "I won't tell on you, Carmella."

She nodded, then turned and opened the door to the pantry. Pulling a stepladder off its hook on the wall, she set it down in front of the shelves in the front left corner of the pantry, the side of the opening of the door.

"I saw Mr. Leland put this up here. Since I know you are trying to help now, I thought it might be important."

She climbed the stepladder and pulled a black cell phone from behind canned goods on the top shelf. Handing it to him she held it back, "You promised."

"I promise."

Releasing the phone to him, he turned it over and looked at it closely. It was a burner phone. Exiting the pantry, he nodded to Carmella and tucked the phone into his pocket and hurried toward the steps leading upstairs. He'd see if he could hook this up to the computer and pull information from it.

Closing the bedroom door, he walked to the small bed on the far wall and sat on the edge. Pulling his duffle bag toward him, he fished inside until he found a pack of cords. Locating the correct end, he inserted it in the phone then found the USB end and plugged it into his computer. Watching as the phone lit up and the little wheel spun on his screen his head swam. This could be the end of their mission and he was eager to get back to headquarters. He was. Yes, he would like to go back home.

Heaving in a deep breath and slowly letting it out, he shook his head muttering, "Damn women."

His computer came to life and a list of numbers began populating his computer screen.

Actually one number, listed over and over and over. It looked to be a phone number of sorts, but different than US numbers. 011 994 13 49803435. He'd give his left nut if he were wrong about this. Looking up the description of telephone numbers in Azerbaitani he instantly noted that this was indeed a foreign number and an Azerbaitani number, too.

Now to find out from Raymond what Zacara's number

was. First to let Gaige know what he'd stumbled on and find out how he wanted this handled. After all, Casper had hired them, and the protocol may be to contact Casper for some of the things they found.

Texting Gaige, he typed out. "I found something I think is a phone number in Azerbaitani. Should I act on it or send it to Casper?"

Within seconds Gaige replied, "Get it to Casper, I'm now out on a mission. Ford is with me, Lincoln is at HQ."

"Roger."

He scrolled through his phone for Casper's number and tapped his name. The first ring sounded within seconds. He'd never met Casper, didn't know what he looked like. Hopefully one day he'd get to meet this man that helped them so much.

"Hawk. How can I help you?"

"I found a burner phone with an Azerbaitani number listed many times on it. Handing it off to you. What would you like me to do with it?"

"I'd like you to find out who's number it is. Put in your report how many times and the dates that number was called. See if Jared can do some hacking and find any texts or voicemails to this phone. I won't have the clearance here to do that. I'll clear what Jared is doing with our contact at the State Department. If you don't hear back from me immediately, it's a go which I expect it will be."

"On it."

"Hawk? Call me as soon as you have something."

"Yes, sir."

Awesome, he'd get to see this through.

36

S he followed Jax up to her parents' room once again and braced herself from flinching when she walked in this time. Relief flooded through her when she entered the bedroom and she didn't break into tears. Progress.

Jax stopped and looked at her, must have been satisfied with what she saw, then walked to the side of the bed and pulled her laptop from her bag. The bed was neatly made, the room was orderly. Jax grinned when she watched her stare at the bed. "We're both former military. Everything neat and tidy." She said as she logged onto her laptop.

Jax sat in the middle of the bed, crossed her legs, then pulled her laptop on her lap and began typing.

Glancing around the room she studied the chair in the corner and thought about pulling it up to the bed, but that seemed too stiff and uncomfortable. Jax looked up from her computer and said, "If it's too hard to be in here we can go back downstairs to the dining room."

Breathing in and letting it out she smiled at Jax, who

she'd actually call her friend. "No, I'm sick of sitting down there."

She sat next to Jax on the bed, crossed her legs also, and opened her laptop and logged on. She wasn't sure what she'd be looking for, but Jax began chatting first. "You know he has feelings for you. It's just hard because of Sarah."

Her stomach plummeted to her feet. "Who's Sarah?"

"His wife."

Black. She couldn't see anything because her world turned black. "What?" She managed to squeak out.

Jax laughed. "I'm busting your chops a little bit. Because I wanted you to see that you have feelings for him, too. Sarah was his wife, but she was killed. It was before I knew him, but I'm told that he was working a mission and Sarah was shot in crossfire. She died in his arms."

"Oh, my gosh, how sad."

"It's why he keeps a distance. But, I can see he's different with you. And, shit, it's been ten years. It's time he moved on."

Roxanne stared across the room thinking about Hawk holding a dying woman that he loved. It was enough to break her heart again.

"Did he tell you about that?"

"No, he doesn't talk about it much. But a long time ago, he told my brother, Jake. He's gone now too. Anyway, Jake told me after Hawk and I had a one-night stand."

Her head spun around so fast she almost fell off the bed. "You and Hawk?"

Jax twisted to look her head on. "It was years ago and only one night and we both knew afterwards that it was a mistake. Dodge knows, and as you can imagine, he isn't all that happy about it. That's why there's a bit of tension between them. But, neither of us has ever looked back or thought about repeating it. My grandfather had just died and I was broken up and crying. Hawk was consoling me, told me he'd lost Sarah, but not specifics and he knew what I was going through. We had a few drinks and one thing led to another. That's it."

She sat staring at Jax, who'd just dropped two huge bombshells on her and typed on her computer as if nothing had been said. Hawk had been married and he'd slept with Jax. How to process this? Of course, both were so long ago that it made little difference. And, since Hawk didn't seem interested in repeating anything with her either, her next thought was that he just had one-night stands. So, it was probably better that she left it where it was and not get any deeper involved.

Her computer chimed that she had an email and Jax said, "I just sent you a link to log on to. You'll need to log on with an active link, so my username and password are also in the email. Once you're there, let me know."

Her senses were a bit dull now and following directions was overwhelming. She sat staring at her email for a moment, the bolded text email from Jax in the top of her inbox and she wondered if she was doing the right thing. Turning to Jax, she asked, "There aren't any pictures of my parents lying dead in here are there?"

Jax's eyes locked on hers. "No. I would have warned you if there were." Closing the lid to her laptop, Jax turned her body so she was facing her. "Look, I know this has all been difficult. I'm impressed with how you're handling it actually. It takes a strong person to cope with everything you're dealing with and other than us, a group of people you just met under strange circumstances, you're doing it without family close by. I just knew Hawk didn't have anything for you to do. I wanted to let him off the hook and save you from being embarrassed or hurt further. I can certainly use the help scouring through the reports, but if it's just too much, lay back and take a nap or play on your phone, I've got this."

She seemed earnest. Their eyes were locked on each other and she saw sincerity and honesty. And she felt proud that Jax thought she was doing a good job. "I can handle it. I just wanted to prepare myself. No more chop busting, okay?"

Jax held her fist out for a fist-bump, then she got back to work.

They searched the reports from the law enforcement agencies on the shootings and the suspected location of where the shooter likely was positioned. The trouble was, the reports she read had the shootings from different locations. That meant that either there was more than one shooter or... Well what? Then she exclaimed, "Holy fuck. I think I know what happened."

She slammed the lid to her laptop, hustled off the bed and flew out the door. Running down the steps it was hard for Jax to keep up with her longer strides. Finding the dining room empty she pulled her phone from her back pocket and texted Hawk.

From upstairs the text could be heard reaching its recipient and she and Jax flew back up the stairs. Her brother Matt's door opened and Dodge, Hawk and Wyatt stepped out. Axel showed up last and she stopped in front of the group of men. Jax, who now had one hand on a hip, still holding her laptop in her other hand barked. "Are you all in there goofing around while we're working?"

Dodge grinned, "We all did our duties and we're

waiting for information so, yeah, we're shooting the breeze."

Jax turned to look at her. "See what I have to put up with? Sometimes, it's fucking irritating."

Dodge stepped forward and tried to put his arm around her shoulders, which she shrugged away. "Not now, Tarzan."

Hawk spoke up next. "Tell us what you've got Roxanne so Jax can stop busting our chops."

Holding up their laptops, Dodge motioned that they go into Matt's room and they all filed in. Matt had a desk so Roxanne set her computer on the desk and pulled up a webpage. "The reports are all over the place as to where the shots came from. But, there are no reports of anyone being seen leaving any of the buildings, running away or otherwise. Secret Service would have had each room facing the capital secured in case the President stepped outside to greet the Prime Minister. It happens. So that leaves this."

She tapped on a couple of links and opened up another page. "These are drones that can shoot up to twenty bullets at a range of 400 feet away. This particular drone was made by the US military in the hopes of diminishing loss of life of our military. However, there have been cases of copycats now on the market." She clicked on another webpage. "And, according to this news report, Azerbaitani has access to these drones from Iran. I think my parents and the Prime Minister were shot by a drone. That means we have to find reports of someone using an electronic device. Or see if there's another way to track the devices controlling drones."

Hawk kneeled and read the articles she'd pulled up. "How do you know about drones?"

"I work with another attorney who is fascinated with them and he sends me articles when he's researching them. Plus, I know some stuff from my dad. With the bullets coming from all angles, it just clicked."

Hawk then turned to leave the room. "I'll contact Gaige and Casper."

37

"**G**reat job, Hawk. We've been able to search our intel on drones; we keep detailed information on drone activity, especially drones such as this. And, we've confirmed that Azerbaitani does indeed have drones that can shoot. They are equipped with machine guns and have a great range. We've been trying to destroy them or capture them when we find them, but it isn't easy to do. They are silent and hard to see. This would be especially true at the time of night the Bowmans and the Prime Minister were in range. The sun had almost set and the duskiness in the sky would make visibility difficult. The biggest question is how they got it here without detection." Casper said.

"Great, one more thing to have to deal with and the fact that factions we aren't even fighting with have this technology makes it even worse." He dragged his hand through his hair, then pinched the bridge of his nose.

"Yes. Luckily for us we have better technology and the means to track. I'll keep in touch with what we find out about how it may have gotten into the country. For the record, investigators have been looking into that theory, but the wheels here turn so slow."

"Roger. Out." Ending his call with Casper, Hawk looked around the room that was actually Brendan Bowman's room. Comfortable, nicely appointed and clean. This whole house was impressive. If Brendan and Matthew were anything like Roxanne, they were an amazing family. His stomach tightened thinking about what couldn't be.

A knock on the door jarred him from his thoughts, "Yeah."

The door opened and Wyatt's head poked in. "Carmella said it's time for supper."

"I'll be right there."

Wyatt disappeared and Hawk heaved himself off the bed and trudged to the bathroom in this room. It appeared the Bowmans at some point in time had retro-fitted each bedroom with its own bathroom. They were small rooms, but were private and comfortable. Washing his hands and splashing water on his face he purposefully forced himself to think about this mission ending and getting his team back without incident. As soon as Casper gave them the signal that they'd completed their mission, they'd be calling on the GHOST plane to come and pick them up. He was more than ready. In his mind. He'd have to work a bit more to keep his stomach from twisting at the thought of leaving. And, right now he was wrestling with how to say goodbye to Roxanne. It seemed cold and hurtful to just walk away. But having a heart to heart with her and saying goodbye seemed messy and complicated.

Toweling his face off and drying his hands he left the

bathroom, walked across the room to the door and stepped out. That's when he ran into Roxanne.

Literally.

She was planted against his body and he noticed three things almost simultaneously. She smelled fantastic. She felt perfect against him. And the little sound she made when they ran into each other was similar to the sounds she made when he was making love to her. It caused his body to react in a way they both felt. Her head tilted up to meet his eyes and he liked that she was taller than many women and didn't have to crane her neck back as far as others. Sarah had only been 5'4". Roxanne easily had five inches or so on her.

Roxanne's hands then grabbed his shirt on either side of his waist and he could feel her hands shaking. She licked her lips and that did it for him. He bent his head and kissed her. She kissed him back and his arms snaked around her body and pulled her fully into his, which made him grow thick and hard.

She moaned and he felt the vibration of it through his entire body and he deepened his kiss, tasting her mouth completely. Sounds of footsteps from below snapped him from his carnal thoughts and he pulled away slightly, looked into her light blue eyes, sure to never forget that color as long as he lived, then whispered, "We're not alone."

She inhaled and stepped away at the same time and he wondered if she felt the loss of heat and solace as much as he did.

Turning to look downstairs he saw no one, but likely whoever was down there saw them kissing and turned to leave. The cat was surely out of the bag now.

"I just relayed your findings on the drones to our contact with the military. He's looking into it now and is impressed."

Clearing her throat lightly she softly replied, "Thank you and I'm happy if I could help. I need the closure."

Oh, his heart just hurt so much more. She'd just been through so much and he was going to be hurting her more. The sharp pain in his stomach was well deserved.

"I'm sure you do. Let's head down to dinner."

He held his hand out for her to precede him, then followed her down the grand staircase and to the dining room.

The delicious aroma of roasted chicken, mashed potatoes and creamed corn reached his nostrils and his mouth watered a bit. He'd have to hit the gym hard when he got home. Carmella made huge meals and he had a hard time curbing how much he partook.

The two chairs left were the one he'd been occupying at the end of the table and the chair to his right. He and Roxanne sat in what now seemed like their usual spots and Carmella began bringing the food out. His stomach growled when she lay freshly baked, still steaming biscuits on the table. Axel had a gluten problem and Mrs. James and her daughter, Kylie, who cooked for GHOST made delicious food for their group, but it was all gluten free. Still tasty, but a real old-fashioned biscuit sounded heavenly now. Poor Axel would need to go without, but there was plenty of food for him to eat.

Wyatt held up his glass of milk and said, "Here's to Roxanne and Jax for figuring out the drones."

Jax held up her water and replied, "To Roxanne, she figured it out."

The group said their cheers and he turned his head toward her, noting how beautiful she was with the hint of pink on her cheeks. "Here's to you, Luna." He said softly and he saw her eyes well with tears, before she looked at her plate.

38

She was going to lose it. She watched as each member of this team, she'd spent the past week and a half with carry their belongings out to the rented SUV's, now parked in the driveway. They'd been given orders to leave, called on their team plane, which she had known nothing about until Jax mentioned it, but they clearly had high security clearances and a lot of money to have their own plane. But as to their name or actual job, she was still in the dark.

The military had confirmed the drone shooting and the bullets matched bullets made on foreign soil, but they were still figuring out how it had made its way into the United States and worse yet, from their perspective, so close to the White House. Security had been ramped up and travel restrictions were now in place on people coming in from certain foreign countries.

Raymond stood alongside her. But he was leaving, too. He was going to live under an assumed name, which she didn't even know. His stay at the first place would likely be short as part of the hiding process would be to move him a few times under different names to ensure his safety. Uncertain as to whether he was still a target, she was grateful that the government was helping him hide, even though that would be a hard life, too.

Jax came to stand beside her and watched with her as Wyatt and Axel stowed their gear in the back of their SUV, then waved and hopped into the vehicle. Dodge walked to Roxanne and held his hand out to shake. "Thank you for your hospitality and assistance with completing our mission. Please know I am truly sorry for your loss."

She smiled at him, this handsome man with his blond hair and light green eyes. Such a contrast to his future wife, but they made a stunning couple. "You're welcome, thank you and come back again if you're ever in Washington, my door will always be open to you all."

He nodded, took Jax's duffle bag from her hands with a little frown from her. "I can offer to help once in a while, let me while you say goodbye."

She winked at him, then let go of her bag and both women watched Dodge walk out of the house and down the sidewalk. "He has a great ass, doesn't he?" Jax said.

She giggled, she'd been thinking it, but would never say it. Instead she replied, "You're a lucky woman, Jax. But then again, he's pretty friggin' lucky, too."

They turned to face each other and Jax hugged her firmly. It felt fantastic to be accepted and appreciated by this strong, smart, beautiful woman.

Jax stood back, "Dodge and I are getting married next weekend. Would you please come to my wedding? I'd love to have you there."

"Are you kidding me? I'd love to be there. Are you sure it won't be awkward?"

The dark-haired beauty shrugged, "Not for me. Promise."

"I promise."

Jax smiled, "I'll text you all the deets." then she turned and strutted down the sidewalk toward Dodge, who stood alongside the SUV waiting for his bride.

Raymond was next, still awkward and unsure, but he stepped in front of her and took her hands in his. Looking at their hands he softly said, "Thank you for keeping me safe. Leland and Kay loved you so much. He was so worried about you being caught up in the middle of this. He's resting easy knowing you're alright."

A single tear rolled down her cheek. "Thank you for saying that. And, thank you for all you did to help Dad out. I know he trusted and appreciated what you did for him and I do, too. Stay safe, Raymond."

He turned and left without another word and her heart squeezed for this unusual man. She genuinely hoped he'd be safe.

"I'm last."

Her heartbeat skipped then sped up as his deep voice floated over her and his scent enveloped her. He came to stand before her and looked into her eyes. "I'm not sure what to say, Roxanne. I don't want to make this harder, but, I can't do...I don't do relationships."

He swallowed and she was mesmerized by his Adam's apple as it moved up and down in his sexy neck. Tears, which had already come to life when saying goodbye to Raymond, trickled down her cheeks and she had to give herself a moment to gather her composure.

"I understand." She didn't, but she did. It still hurt though.

"You have my number, if you need anything, call me. I mean it. I will always have your six."

"Thank you, Hawk. It was a pleasure getting to know you."

He gently touched his lips to hers and she tried closing her mind off from the pain. She stepped back and as he walked down the sidewalk, she closed the front door and leaned against the back of it as she let the tears flow.

Swiping them away, she took in several deep breaths and allowed herself the time, once again, to grieve. After all, she might see him at Jax and Dodge's wedding. Though Jax told her that if a mission came up, Hawk would likely take it first so he wasn't around for the wedding. Dodge and Hawk still weren't totally comfortable with each other and it would keep tensions low.

One final deep breath and she pushed herself off the door, set the alarm on the panel to the right of the door and went to the kitchen to find Carmella and see when the new carpeting would be installed. Get back to normal - that would be her new mantra.

"Carmella, I've set the alarm and I'll go up and pull the sheets from the beds."

"No, Miss Roxy, that's my job."

"Carmella, I need to stay busy, I'm doing this much, then I think I'll take a long nap."

39

"Nice job on your report, Hawk." Gaige said as he read from his computer screen.

"Thanks." He sat with a thud and stared across the conference room at GHOST headquarters. One of their lower levels was their conference room/computer center, gun range, and medical clinic. The level below this one was their parking garage. The Southern Mission style home had been refurbished before they moved in, just for their needs in mind. Most of the members lived here with nice sized rooms and personal bathrooms on the second story. Sophie had now moved in with Gaige in his rooms, but Jax rarely stayed here anymore since Dodge had a home just a few miles away at the foot of Lynyrd Station on the Hill, which was the mountain owned by Ford. Lincoln and his wife, Skye, also lived at the foot of the Hill while Ford and his family lived on top of the Hill. But, he was still here and planned on being here until he either died or had to retire from GHOST.

"You're quiet this week. More quiet than usual Hawk, what's on your mind?"

"Nothing."

Gaige moved to sit at his left at the conference table, but sat quietly, which he was fine with. He didn't know what was eating at him. He was just out of sorts.

Gaige leaned back in his chair and let out a long breath. "When I saw Sophie again it rattled me to no end. You were there, you saw it all. It didn't take long before I knew she was the one. Someone special in my life that I could not live without."

Filling his lungs till they burned he let his breath out slowly. "Jax has a big mouth."

Chuckling, Gaige said, "Actually Wyatt does."

"Fucker."

"That special person only comes along once in a lifetime."

"My special person came along and died in my arms."

"And here you are, given a second chance at something special and you're moping around and surly because you're afraid to give it a try."

"I'm not moping around."

"The fuck you're not."

Standing abruptly, he stalked from the room. He should have known better; he wasn't fit for company now and should have stayed in his room. Jabbing the button on the wall to open the elevator he stared at it while waiting and as soon as the doors whooshed open, without looking he stomped inside.

"Whoa, excuse me." Wyatt remarked as he stepped back instead of out of the elevator.

"You have a big fucking mouth, Wyatt."

Shaking his head, Wyatt stepped off the elevator but left a parting comment. "And you're a dumbass, Hawk.

Fucking stupid. I think I'll give Roxanne a call and see if she's interested in a bit of Wyatt."

The doors closed before Hawk could pull them open but at this moment, his anger was at an all-time high.

The doors opened on the first floor and he stepped out without thinking that he wanted to go up one more floor. The aroma of flowers and the chatter of female voices reached him. Giggling and activity, both things he'd like to avoid. He turned to get back on the elevator, but the doors had already closed.

"Hey, Hawk, come and help us with these big boxes please." Jax called down the hall.

"Look, Jax, I'm just not in the mood for..."

"Just come and help us move this one box, its heavy and it's falling apart, I just need a little muscle. Then you can go back to pouting."

"Jesus Chr...I'm not pouting."

She planted her hands on her slender hips and glared at him enough that he stomped toward her. When he'd entered the foyer area of the large home, they all shared he stopped quickly at the sheer chaos he saw. Boxes were strewn everywhere, flowers, ribbons, and some flimsy looking material. Ford's wife, Megan, Lincoln's wife, Skye, Sophie, Mrs. James, Kylie and Jax all stood amongst the rubble.

"Holy fuck, what is all of this?"

"In case you've forgotten, I'm getting married tomorrow. This box right here needs to be slid over to that wall. It's the arbor we're putting up in a little bit and stringing flowers and lights around. But we can't lift the damned thing and we've got a lot of stuff to do today, so please help a girl out."

Heaving out a big breath, he bent over and scooted the

big box to the far wall, giving the ladies the room they needed to decorate. They all clapped and whistled as he did it and he actually smiled a little.

"Is that it?" He asked as he stood.

"Yeah, thanks."

"Where's your husband-to-be? Shouldn't he be helping with this heavy shit?"

Jax laughed. "Don't be a grouch. He's in the shooting range."

"Fucker." He huffed out as he started climbing the stairs.

The women started chattering again and Jax was directing the show. It looked like a total fucking mess from this vantage point, but it wasn't his worry.

Axel stepped from his room as Hawk walked to his. "Those women still making a mess down there?"

"Yes. Don't know how they'll pull it all off, but not my worry."

Axel shook his head and began walking to the stairs. "See you're still a grouch."

He was sick of being called a grouch. Dammit. Why hadn't he been sent on a fucking mission by now? He'd hoped to avoid this whole thing. He wasn't jealous, he just felt out of place. Out of sorts. Out of control. He'd never had such a moody spell in his entire life, and it didn't sit well.

Stripping out of his clothing, he donned a pair of running shorts and a sleeveless shirt. A good hard run might help him clear his mind.

Jogging down the stairs quickly, he turned and navigated the mess on the floor while the women were wrapping Christmas Lights in that flimsy material and to his joy, he was largely unnoticed.

Skipping out the backdoor, he left the compound, and hit the back streets behind the house to start out on his jog. Shoving earphones in his ears, he hit his jogging playlist on his phone, stuck his phone in his jogging armband, and took off at a rapid pace. He'd run himself tired then try and sleep after he showered. It had been a couple of weeks since he'd actually slept good, so time for a fresh start on moving forward.

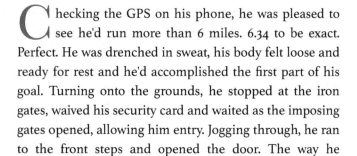

Checking the GPS on his phone, he was pleased to see he'd run more than 6 miles. 6.34 to be exact. Perfect. He was drenched in sweat, his body felt loose and ready for rest and he'd accomplished the first part of his goal. Turning onto the grounds, he stopped at the iron gates, waived his security card and waited as the imposing gates opened, allowing him entry. Jogging through, he ran to the front steps and opened the door. The way he smelled, the women would surely leave him alone.

Swiping the sweat from his brow with the back of his forearm, he opened the massive front door and stepped inside.

That's when his heart stopped, and his world changed.

40

There he stood, Hawk, sweaty from a run, his sleeveless shirt clung to every ab perfectly. What she couldn't see outlined was still in her memories and likely always would be. His hair had been shoved back from his face with his hands, the grooves his fingers made still fresh. His broad shoulders looked even broader as his shirt clung to his narrowed waist. He was positively swoon worthy. The tattoos on both arms, full sleeves of intricate designs and woven together. Normally, that would not be appealing to her, but on Hawk, it was damned sexy.

He froze, his eyes locked on hers and it was as if no one else was in the room. She knew they were of course, and she'd been in the midst of being given the rundown on how everything would pull together when he walked in.

Her cheeks burned bright red and her heart hammered in her chest. "Hi."

It was lame, but it was all she could muster at that moment. She hadn't expected to see him, not this afternoon, maybe tomorrow, and certainly not as if he lived here. Coming in from a run with all these people present. In this monstrous house.

"Hi. I wasn't expecting you to be here." Her heart dropped. He didn't want to see her? Then he finished his sentence. "But I'm glad you are." His lips turned up the slightest little bit. He swiped at a trickle of sweat that rolled down his temple then continued. "Let me take a shower then I'll come back down."

She nodded, still a bit confused about the sleeping arrangements or who actually lived in this house. She'd only been here about twenty minutes and the instant she walked in she was pulled into the wedding set up and meeting these other amazing women. Then a string of lights was handed to her and directions to wrap them in gossamer and tie the material with pink ribbons.

Jax walked over to her, "I forgot to tell you he didn't leave on a mission. So, he's home for now, and the wedding."

"Home?" She cleared her throat and tried to get her brain to catch up. "He lives here?"

Jax cocked her head to the right and bit her bottom lip. "I guess we haven't really told you anything about us." She motioned to include all of the women in the room. "Before I speak out of turn, let me make sure Gaige will allow me to tell you what we're all about. I'll be right back. You keep wrapping lights with Sophie."

Jax walked down the hall to the left, pushed a button on the wall and, holy moley, an elevator opened and she stepped in. Blinking to make sure her eyes were working she heard Sophie giggle next to her. "It's an amazing place. When I first got here, I was amazed."

"Right." She said absently. Turning to look at Sophie, she asked, "Do you live here?"

"Yes. I'm with Gaige, we're getting married later this year. Probably here like Jax and Dodge are."

"Okay."

She turned to look at Megan and Skye. "Do you live here, too?"

Megan laughed. "No, we live a few miles away at Lynyrd Station on the Hill."

"Okay. I don't know what that is."

Skye replied. "It's Ford and Megan's mountain just out of town. Megan and Ford live at the top of the mountain. Lincoln and I live at the bottom and so do Jax and Dodge. Actually, you're welcome to stay with Linc and I if you don't want to go to a hotel while you're here. Unless you're staying here with Hawk."

"No. I mean, I'm not staying here with Hawk. And I don't want to put you out or anything."

Jax appeared from the elevator and stepped to her. "So Gaige gave the go ahead to tell you some things, but I actually think Hawk should tell you, so if you don't mind helping out until he comes back down, I'd appreciate it. We don't have a lot of time and we have a fair amount of stuff to finish."

"Of course not. I'm at your service." Her head was whirling with information. It seemed to be the norm these days.

She and Sophie finished wrapping a string of lights then she climbed the ladder on the right side of the foyer and in front of the upper railing of the staircase, holding the gossamer covered lights to the bottom of the railing as Skye fastened it on the back side.

Then Skye raced to the other end of the railing where

Jax was holding another strand of lights to fasten them for her.

The string of material covered lights trailed across the foyer entrance, but the design was already taking shape. Climbing down from the ladder, she walked across the large area to the other end of the lights and looked up. Megan and Sophie were wrapping the railing with Madevilla Vines with gorgeous pink flowers on them. She smiled when she realized the pink in the flowers matched the pink ribbons they'd wrapped around the gossamer and lights. She never would have guessed Jax loved pink.

The elevator at the end of the hall opened and Dodge popped out with Wyatt. "Okay, what do you need me to do?" he asked.

Then he spotted her. "Hey, Roxanne, you made it. Awesome."

She smiled as he genuinely seemed happy she was here. "Hi Dodge, thanks for having me."

He walked to Jax, who was moving a ladder and took it from her. "Let me help out just a bit, Little Mama."

Jax gave him a look, then relinquished her hold on the ladder and let him move it to the opposite side of the room where they'd hang the other end of the lights, criss-crossing them in the middle. He climbed the ladder and Jax handed him the end of the string of lights and a fastener and she had to admit, as it was coming together, it was going to be gorgeous.

Dodge climbed down and Jax said, "The rest of you guys can get up here and help out now that your workouts are finished. Get them up here, Tarzan."

He chuckled but pulled his phone from his pocket. Seemingly sending a text, it wasn't long before Axel showed up. Then three men she hadn't met joined the group. Ford, Lincoln and Gaige were introduced to her before Jax put them to work.

Finally Hawk began descending the massive staircase and she thought her heart would skip right out of her chest. He looked simply fantastic freshly showered, wearing nice fitting jeans and a clean black three button plaquette shirt. Holy sexiness right there.

41

W alking down the steps his stomach fluttered and his heart beat so fast he thought it would stop. Literally. Looking at Roxanne as she stood amongst flowers and flimsy material caused his mind to picture her in a wedding dress. She'd be a beautiful bride. She was a beautiful woman, even in sweatpants and a t-shirt.

She turned and her eyes landed on him and he felt it all the way through his body. Every inch of him came alive. Focusing his mind on not falling down the stairs he looked ahead and tried gaining some control over his mind. She really had him wrapped up.

Just as he landed on the floor Gaige stepped up to him and quietly said, "You should tell her what we are. Swear her to secrecy, but I assume as an attorney, she understands confidentiality very well."

He nodded at his friend and boss, received a slap on the shoulder and a grin, then Gaige dove back into the fray of helping prepare the area for a wedding. Chairs were being delivered at the moment and would need to be set up as soon as all the lights were hung.

Making his way to Roxanne he smiled at her. "Hi. Again. I didn't know you were coming for the wedding, but as I said, I'm glad you did."

She smiled and his stomach fluttered again. "I couldn't say no to Jax." She leaned in, "She's a little scary when she gets her head set on something."

"Don't I know it." He chuckled, but then saw her smile fade and her eyes look down at the ground.

Tucking his fingers under her chin he gently pulled her face up to look at him. "Hey, what happened there?"

She swallowed, inhaled deeply and said, "Jax told me. About you two. And I know it was long ago, but I guess I'm feeling like odd man out here."

Nodding he said, "Okay, well, it was long ago and a mistake never to be repeated. Look at what's going on here, she's getting married."

"I know. And, it's so stupid but I guess it just hurts a little."

He reached for her hand and tugged her to the kitchen. "Come on, let me give you a tour and tell you about what we do here."

Walking into the aromatic kitchen, the sizzling sounds of supper cooking, the smell of fresh baked bread filtering through the room and Mrs. James and Kylie chopping and stirring food, they both stopped and smiled.

Mrs. James said, "Hi Hawk, Roxanne. Are you looking for something to eat?"

He responded, "No, I'm showing Roxanne the house."

Kylie responded, "Oh, it's a beautiful house, enjoy your tour. Dinner will be ready in a half-hour."

Roxanne sweetly responded. "Oh, thank you, it smells fantastic."

He tugged her to the dining room, just through the door on the right and proudly proclaimed. "Dining room. As you can imagine, we take our big meals here, but it's seldom we're all in attendance. Tonight and tomorrow will be special."

He pointed to the trees outside the window. "Jax and Josh, her twin brother, he'll be here later tonight, he went to pick up their mother, Pilar, planted the larger tree on the left for their brother Jake and their father as a memorial. Both of them died working with us. We're all members of GHOST - Government Hidden Ops Specialty Team. We're a trained, highly specialized civilian special forces team. We work mostly for the government and as you know our work is highly secretive. We go in and do things the government can't do. We try to do things legally, but we do push the line once in a while to complete our missions. That's why we were in Washington working to figure out who killed your parents and the Prime Minister."

She turned to look at him and studied his face for a few moments. "And most of you live here?"

"Yes. This house was purchased and remodeled for us. Gaige owns GHOST, his father before him. Some of the team live off-site, that's certainly an option. But, Wyatt, Axel, Josh, Gaige, Sophie and I, we all live here."

Nodding she turned and looked at the trees outside. "And Jax's brother and father were killed on missions?"

"Yes."

"Who's the other tree for?"

"Adam. Dodge's son was killed when he was a toddler."

Her hand flew to her stomach and he saw her swallow rapidly. "That's so sad."

"Yes. It is."

For long moments Roxanne looked out the window, then softly asked, "Why didn't you plant a tree for Sarah?"

It was like getting punched in the stomach. His breath whooshed from his lungs and he was unable to say anything for a long time. Finally, she turned and looked into his eyes. "It would be a nice way to memorialize her life."

Clearing his throat, he decided to change the subject. "Let me finish showing you around." Walking back through the kitchen and to the foyer amid the hustle and bustle, he turned her to the right and the formal living room.

"Wow, this is gorgeous."

"It is, but nearly ever used. We don't lounge around in here at all. But, it's here if we need it white carpet and all."

Turning her around, he led her through the side of the foyer and to the next door on the right, which was Gaige's office. Opening the door, he said, "This is Gaige's office and where he takes sensitive phone calls and lines up our missions."

"This home is so beautiful."

"Says the woman who lives in a palatial home."

She shrugged and smiled slightly, and he was grateful the mood had lifted. Leading her down the hall on the opposite side of the foyer, he waived his security card and waited for the elevator light to signal is was okay to open the door. At the signal, he opened it, then for Roxanne to step inside.

"Below are two levels. One is where we work, the other is the garage. Both floors are bulletproof in case something happens. So, the floors are bunkers in case we ever have to be in lockdown for any period of time.

"This is simply amazing. I never would have guessed."

"That's the point."

The doors slid open and they stepped into the hallway. The frosted glass across the hall that hid their workroom was lit, even though no one would be inside. "He opened the door with his key card and stepped aside for her to enter. He watched her for a moment, amazed at what she was seeing, and taking it all in, then he wrapped his arms around her and kissed her lips. It was as if all the tension from this week faded away with her in his arms. The instant her arms wrapped around his waist and pulled him closer to her, his mind forgot this past week and settled on spending time with Roxanne. As much as he could. Maybe he'd give this relationship thing a chance. That was if she wanted to.

42

His lips were soft yet commanding, his strong arms wrapped around her and made her feel protected and cared for and excited. She couldn't deny excited. She'd missed him this week as much as she tried to pretend otherwise. But, her heart broke a little the day he left. The only thing that got her through this week was knowing she was coming here and the hope that she'd see him. Though, in her mind it was much different.

Pulling away slightly he lay his forehead on hers, his breathing was ragged and she could feel his heart beat so close to hers.

"I missed you." He whispered.

Her heart raced and she felt a thousand butterflies take flight in her stomach. "I missed you, too."

He pulled back slightly, "Let me finish showing you around, then we have to be present for the rehearsal; and I think they're planning on going into town to the Copper Cup where Dodge and Jax first met and where he actually proposed to her. It'll be fun. You and I haven't been able to just go out and have fun."

"No, we haven't and that sounds nice. I'll need to go back to the hotel first and change though."

"I'll take you to the hotel. I'll bring you back there afterward, too."

She smiled. "You're being a gentleman. I didn't realize badasses were gentlemen, too."

"Sweetheart, we are so much more than meets the eye. My Ma would have kicked my ass if she thought I wasn't a gentleman."

"Aww, you listen to your ma, that's awesome."

His face grew serious. "She's gone now, both of my parents are. Just like you."

Laying her hand on his cheek, she whispered, "I'm so sorry. It sucks."

He kissed the tip of her nose, "Yes, it does." Turning to the door, he took her hand in his and led her down the hall to another room.

"This is our shooting range." Flipping a light switch, she saw a dark room, with thick padding and tables lined up in front of the range. At the back of the range were bolsters of rubber to catch the bullets and overhead, electronic clips to hold targets. There were no casings on the floor and everything was neat. Flack jackets were neatly hung to the left side of the room.

"Wow, this is impressive."

He smiled and she could see his pride. Motioning with his hand to the door, she turned and walked out as he flipped the lights off and closed the door. They traced their path down the hallway, past the computer center they'd kissed in and to a small door at the end of the hall.

He opened it up and the lights clicked on. A small medical room appointed with a table, shelves with supplies like cotton balls, and ointments and rubber gloves in a cabinet on the wall.

"This is our medical room. Gaige and Wyatt were medics in the service and they take care of small things in here and on missions."

"Wow, I had no idea."

"They don't brag about it, but they're pretty fucking good. On a recent mission, Dodge got shot and Wyatt had to stabilize him. Jax took over applying pressure while Wyatt drove him to the hospital. It wasn't a bad injury, but it was great Wyatt was there."

Leaving the medical room, he walked again with her hand in his to the elevator, waived his key card and waited for her to step in when the doors opened. Pushing the button labeled Gar she could feel them go down a floor. They stepped out into the neatest garage she'd ever seen. And that was saying something because her dad was neat as a pin.

"Wow, this is impressive. Which car is yours? Or is that top secret?"

He chuckled and she liked the sound. A lot. "I have the Black Pickup on the right and toward the back. I also have the bike right next to it."

Both vehicles were newer, neat and clean and parked perfectly. Actually all of the vehicles in the garage were.

"See, that just proves you're a badass."

Chuckling he shook his head then turned them to the elevator, repeating the card waiving and button pushing the doors closed and within seconds he had her in his arms again. He smelled fantastic and the firmness of his body against hers was more than a turn on. She could feel her body respond in every pore. His lips were soft while his tongue plunged into her mouth and explored. He acted like a starving man and she was his sustenance.

Her arms wrapped around his shoulders, pulling him to her as much as she could but the elevator stopped, and they instinctively pulled away as the doors were opening. Wyatt stood in the hall with a grin on his face a mile wide. "OooWee look at you two go at it."

Taking her hand in his he brushed past Wyatt and in a low growl said, "Fucker."

Wyatt laughed out loud and stepped into the elevator. She could hear his laughter as it faded in the metal box on its descent.

They stopped at the top of the railing and looked down at the decorated foyer, which was stunning. Jax had a vision and no doubt she'd be one in her dress as well. The aroma from the fresh cut flowers thickened in the air, the boxes and bags that held the ribbon, gossamer and flowers had all been cleaned up and Dodge, Axel and Gaige were placing the white wooden chairs in the open area. It was going to be a gorgeous wedding. They stood together silently, watching the activity below and she wondered what he was thinking, but he said nothing and she didn't ask. She hoped he wasn't feeling a bit blue that Jax was getting married or thinking of Sarah. That was just her little jealous self and, likely a bit of insecurity coming out of her, too.

He tugged on her hand a bit and she turned to look up at him. "Let's finish this tour before the rehearsal starts" he said.

"Okay." She smiled at him and hoped he was okay. The

first door on the left after the railing, Hawk pointed to and said, "That's Wyatt's rooms."

Pointing across the hall to a white door, matching all the other doors in the home, he explained, "That's Axel's rooms." Moving to the last door at the end of the hall he waived his card and the door unlocked. "These are my rooms." Opening the door, he stepped back and let her step inside first. The decor was just as beautiful as the rest of the house, the color palette was earth tones in browns, tans, and cream. The walls of the room were a deep brown suede paint and a plush tan area rug lay on the floor. The sofa was cream colored with varying brown pillows and a soft brown throw draped across the back.

A large painting of a tiger hung above the sofa and a large television set hung on the wall across from it. Just past the sofa and into the room a bit further was the massive four poster bed in dark mahogany with a beautiful damask duvet cover in the same color palette. She moved further into the room and saw at the far wall a set of doors on the right of the bed, which looked like the closet. On the opposite side of the room was a single door and upon further inspection was a gorgeous bathroom with a tiled shower and glass doors, granite counters and plush towels.

"Wow, this is an amazing place to live." She couldn't decide what the most beautiful part of the room was.

"It's incredibly nice to live here. Mrs. James and Kylie keep everything clean and keep us organized and fed."

She turned to look at him, "I assume all of the rooms are this nice."

"Yes, though we were able to pick our own colors if we wanted, so some of the team had specific ideas for their rooms; I didn't care and told the designer to do what she wanted. I guess she thought I was wild."

"Hmm." She walked to him and tipped her head up to gaze into his eyes. The green was deeper now, probably due to the colors surrounding him. "I'd say animal magnetism more likely. Tiger fits you."

43

Their phones both began signaling incoming texts and they both ignored them, they were so engrossed in their kiss. At least he was engrossed in the way she felt. The way she smelled, she was intoxicating.

His phone began again and he had to take it. Business called. "Sorry, Luna, I've got to take this."

She stepped back and smiled at him, "I understand."

He watched her pull her phone from her back pocket, then he pulled his from his pocket and read the text. "I'm sorry, I know I told you that I'd take you to the hotel, but Gaige is calling a meeting to discuss a client. I have to go down."

She pecked his lips, "No worries. I can get an Uber."

"You can take my truck if you like."

She giggled. "It's okay, Hawk. I don't know the town very well and I'm fine taking an Uber. I do it all the time. Really."

He grimaced, for so many reasons. He wanted to be with her, he wanted to take her to and from the hotel and spend as much time as he could with her. He wasn't even sure how long she was staying. They had so many things to discuss.

"Come on. Jax wants me downstairs to help with something and you have a meeting." She tugged his hand and he reluctantly followed her to the door. They took the stairs down to the main level and he felt good walking with her at his side. The women were cleaning up the boxes and bags that had contained the plethora of items they had needed to decorate, but it was all coming together now.

Jax saw them coming down and said to Roxanne, "I could use your help making the bows for the chairs."

Roxanne giggled and held up her hands. "Bow making at your service."

At the bottom of the steps, he kissed her lightly and whispered. "I'll see you later. I don't know how long our meeting will be."

"Go on, I'll be fine."

He walked down the hallway and could feel her watching him. This thing they had between them was strong. It was a pull or a blending that he couldn't explain but he liked it.

Getting off the elevator at the conference room level, he walked into the room to find everyone in the room but Dodge and Jax. They were naturally off and actually Josh should be too, but he was here. Walking to Josh and shaking his hand, he said, "I haven't seen you in a few weeks. Nice to have you back."

"It's nice to be back, Hawk. I hear there are some changes or should I say an addition?"

He shook his head and grinned. "She's not an addition exactly. I'm not sure what we're doing."

Josh grinned, "Fair enough."

Gaige walked to the table and plugged in the conference speaker. "Okay, listen up. Casper wants to update us on the Bowman matter and says he has news."

Tapping the speaker, the phone on the other end rang once before Casper's voice came on. "Hello, Gaige."

"Casper, I have Hawk, Josh, Wyatt, Axel, Sophie, Lincoln and Ford with me. Jax and Dodge are preparing to get married."

"Hello everyone and send my congratulations to Jax and Dodge."

Murmurings of hello were heard then Casper jumped right in. "We just got some intel from the TSA that an Azerbaitani citizen just flew into Indiana from Washington. It seems too coincidental to be, well, a coincidence, so I wanted to alert you. Not sure who he's following or why, but I'm sending you pictures we retrieved from the airport surveillance cameras and a camera at the car rental place. He stuck out for two reasons. The case he's carrying is a hard-sided case of some sort, he carried it on, and kept it close to him according to airport personnel. And then somehow breezed through customs without having his case checked. But, he has nothing else with him. No suitcase, etc. A passenger called and was worried about his behavior. Since 9/11 passengers are on high alert to unusual activity."

Hawk looked at his teammates. "Seems like someone is coming to do a job and get out of town."

Casper responded. "Exactly."

Their phones pinged and each of them looked at the text Casper had just sent. Hawk's heart damned near stopped as he looked at the picture, though grainy, of a man who looked remarkably like Raymond Bowman. "Fuck." He muttered.

Trapped between wanting to get as much information as he could and warning Roxanne to stay at the house, he quickly asked, "Do you happen to know where Roxanne is right now?"

Casper responded as his teammates looked at him like he sprouted a second head. "I'm not keeping tabs on her, but I assume she's at home."

He inhaled deeply. "She's here. She got in about two hours ago. What time did this man come into town?"

Papers could be heard shuffling. "About two hours ago. What airline brought Roxanne in?"

"I'll find out."

Looking at his teammates, he said, "She was going to run back to the hotel, I've got to stop her."

Wyatt looked at him and said, "Go, we'll fill you in."

Practically running to the door, he hopped on the elevator and pulled his phone up to text her.

"Don't leave the house. I'll explain when I see you, on my way up now."

Riding the elevator up felt like digging through hard rock by hand, he couldn't make it go any faster. Staring at his phone willing her to respond his stomach felt like he had hot stones laying in the bottom. Bile rose in his throat and his skin grew damp as his temperature rose.

The doors finally opened, and he raced to the foyer only to find it empty. "God dammit."

Looking at his phone again he saw his text say, "undeliverable."

"Fuck." He practically yelled it.

His thumbs never worked so fast. Scrolling to his

contacts, he found Jax's name, tapped her picture and began walking to the elevator.

"Hawk, I'm getting ready for..."

"Jax, where's Roxanne?"

"Whoa, got it bad big guy?"

"Fuck Jax, she's in danger. Some fuckwad from Azerbaitani is here in Indiana, came in at the same time as Roxanne from Washington."

"Shit. She went back to the hotel."

"Dammit. What hotel is she at?"

"She's staying at the Breeze Inn. And, you know it's the only place in town besides the Motel. She'll be too close to him."

"Fuck. I'm on my way there. Keep trying to get in touch with her. My text didn't go through."

He didn't wait for a reply, she'd be on it, he knew her too well. Jabbing the elevator button, he jumped in the second the doors slid open and jabbed the button to go down. He could barely breathe thinking about losing her. It was more than he could bear, not now, not again. Not. Again.

44

Sitting in the back of the Uber she'd called, Roxanne watched as the scenery past by her window. It was pretty here, much prettier than Georgetown. The town was small, but quaint, the businesses in town were well-kept and clean, despite being older. The residents were likely just as nice as the people she'd met today.

A smile formed on her lips as she thought about Hawk and the fact that he'd been so happy to see her. It made all the pain of this week worth it. Almost. The other women she'd met today genuinely seemed sweet and friendly. Beauties, too, all of them. It was slightly intimidating, but only because they knew each other and had developed a strong friendship and she was just coming into the fold. But they welcomed her, asked her about herself and her life and acted as though they really wanted to know her. When was the last time other women welcomed her into their fold? Oh, yeah, never.

Pulling up to the hotel, she signed her name on the

app when the Uber driver, James, handed her his phone. Tapping to leave him a tip, she smiled. "Thank you."

"You're welcome. You may get a survey, please leave me a good review, I'd appreciate it."

"You've got it."

Opening her door she smiled as the fresh aroma of roses reached her nose. Looking around she saw the hotel had rose bushes surrounding the entrance. The gorgeous reds and whites blended together to create a cheery and fragrant entrance. The Uber driver opened the trunk and pulled her suitcase out. Handing it to her he grinned, "Thank you, Miss Bowman."

Giggling she responded, "Thank you, James."

Pulling her suitcase behind her she stepped into the hotel lobby and waited to check in. Glancing around to see the quaint but clean area, she noted a brown leather sofa and two side chairs with earth toned checks on them. Whimsy and colorful. The back area had a breakfast room, so likely they'd serve breakfast . That took care of that worry. The man in front of her in line turned to leave, he looked at her and nodded, then she watched him walk to the elevators. That's when she saw him.

A man who looked eerily close to Raymond briefly stepped off the elevator then back on. She lifted her had to wave to him, but stopped, remembering he was in witness protection now, and likely not anywhere near here. What would the odds be? She didn't even know his new name so she couldn't ask. She'd certainly keep her eyes open though.

"May I help you?" The clerk asked.

"Yes, sorry, I thought I saw someone I knew. Roxanne Bowman, I have a reservation."

The clerk ran her credit card, wrote down her room

number, tucked a key card into an envelope, then handed her the envelope. "Breakfast is from 6:00 a.m. till 9:00 a.m. Coffee and water are free all day, right over there." She pointed to the coffee station next to the breakfast area and just to the left of the sofa and chairs.

"Go up the elevator and your room is on the right."

"Thank you." Roxanne headed to the elevators, suitcase in tow.

Checking the time on her phone she saw that she had an hour to get ready for the rehearsal. She needed to wash the travel muck off of her and feel refreshed, so first thing she'd do is jump in the shower.

Opening the door to her room, she was delighted to see it was bright and airy. The large windows looked out on the mountains in the back and she wondered if one of them was Lynyrd Station on the Hill.

Pulling her toiletry bag off the top of her suitcase, she immediately went into the bathroom and started the shower running while she pulled her shampoo and conditioner and other items from her bag.

Stepping into the shower she enjoyed the feel of the warm water as it enveloped her in its cleaning and soothing properties. Today was a new day and she felt like she was getting a new start on life. A good one.

Taking all the time she wanted, she shampooed, washed, shaved her legs, used an exfoliator on her body and took just a couple of minutes to make her body relax.

Stepping from the shower she thought she heard someone pounding on doors down the hall and hoped it wouldn't be a rowdy group tonight. Drying off and walking out to her room she pulled her pink and black tie-dyed palazzo pants and a black tank top from her bag. These clothes traveled well.

She spent time drying her hair, putting on her makeup and felt she'd pulled off looking fresh. At least she felt clean.

Grabbing her phone, she looked at the time and saw that her phone battery had died. "Shit. All the roaming, I'd forgotten to charge it."

Picking up her purse, she ensured she had a battery pack with her and the cords, draped her purse over her shoulder, grabbed her key card and exited her room.

As she waited for the elevator she pulled her cord out, plugged it into the battery pack, the other end to her phone and turned it on. She stepped on the elevator and the weirdest feeling sent a chill down her spine. She was alone on the elevator, but a sense of dread almost made her stop the elevator and go back up. But it stopped and the doors opened, and she stepped out. That's when all hell broke loose.

She spotted Hawk running toward her, Jax and Dodge behind him. Her smile faltered as she wondered why they were all here. Then, from the corner of her eye, she saw the man who looked like Raymond, step from the dark breakfast room, gun pointed at her and shoot.

The burning sensation that swam through her stomach caused her to buckle but her eyes watched as Hawk pulled his weapon and shot the man several times. Bang. Bang. Bang. Bang. Bang.

45

He was about to lose his shit. He kept shooting that son-of-a-bitch. He'd shoot until he had no more bullets.

"Hawk!" Dodge yelled. "I got him. Go."

He turned and saw Dodge shake his head and he realized he had to snap out of it.

Glancing at Roxanne, her hand over her stomach, blood on her fingers and Jax holding her head in her lap was his worst nightmare coming true. Again.

He ran to Roxanne, his voice barely recognizable as he yelled to Jax, "Call an ambulance."

He quickly assessed Roxanne's condition. He lay his fingers on her neck to feel for a pulse, relief flooded through him when she had one. Jax pulled away and he took her place, feeling for an exit wound, he found none. That wasn't good. There was still a bullet in her, and it likely bounced around a bit.

"Roxanne, baby, tell me you're still with me."

He patted her cheeks to wake her up, she was likely shocked plus any blood loss inside that they couldn't see would affect her consciousness. He pulled her top from her pants and looked at the wound. He wished Wyatt or Gaige were here to make a quick assessment. The small hole, ringed with blood marred her perfect skin and the sight of it nearly made him vomit. He'd seen plenty of these in his time, he'd had a couple himself, but this was Roxanne and he couldn't separate Sarah's death from what was happening right this damned minute.

"Roxanne, please wake up."

"Hawk?" She tried moving, then she groaned and moved her hand to her stomach again. "Ouch." She lay her head back in his lap as he smoothed her hair from her face.

"What happe..."

"You're going to be just fine. For the time being, you are safe and an ambulance is on the way."

"He shot me. Raymond."

"It's not Raymond." Jax said as she kneeled. "He looks a lot like Raymond though."

Sirens wailed outside and Hawk whispered, "The ambulance is here, Luna. You're going to be alright."

Two EMTs ran into the hotel carrying totes and canvas bags and pulling a gurney. Once they reached Roxanne one of them looked at him. "You're going to need to give us room, sir."

He bent down and kissed her lips lightly. "I'll be right here."

Her pale eyes opened briefly and locked on his before closing again. But her lips turned up just a bit before he was pushed aside for them to work on her. He stood alongside as they stopped the bleeding, assessed her vitals, lifted her onto the gurney, and talked into their phones giving the data to an unknown person on the other end of the line. He followed them out and one of them said, "You can't ride with us, sir."

"Yeah, I can," he said and pushed past them and hopped inside.

He sat in the corner, but he took her cold hand in his and tried sending his life force to her. Anything he could do, he'd do it. No question about it.

The EMT in the back with him continued to take her vitals and call in information to the hospital. She was so fair on any given day, but now, she looked scary pale and she lay so still. The only movement was when they hit a bump or turned a corner and her body naturally shifted. He swallowed repeatedly to keep himself from vomiting, and maybe just sane. He wouldn't, just couldn't, let his mind go back to Sarah. His mantra was, "She's going to be fine."

The ambulance turned into the hospital parking lot and drove to the emergency entrance where a garage door opened allowing them access.

Once the door was closed, the driver stopped the ambulance and jumped out. The EMT prepped Roxanne to move her, unlocked the gurney from its supports while the driver pulled the backdoors opened and pulled the gurney to the end of the vehicle. He squeezed her hand one last time before the EMT jumped out and the two men drew the gurney the rest of the way out and locked the legs once they were extended. He scrambled from the back and followed them into the hospital where they were greeted by two nurses and a doctor.

One of the nurses addressed him. "Sir, you'll need to stay in the waiting area now. I'll take you there."

He watched as they ran down a short hallway and turned into a room at the end with Roxanne. His stomach lurched at the thought that he may not see her again. Tears sprang to his eyes and the nurse took his arm and said, "She's in good hands. The best."

He swallowed and nodded, knowing words would likely make him cry like a baby. She led him to a room, not far away, but it felt like miles right now. He sat alone in this small room, with three chairs and two tables piled with magazines and a television with the weather channel on but no sound. Sitting in a chair he leaned forward with his elbows on his knees and lay his face in his hands, trying to breath steadily in and out while repeating to himself, "She's in good hands."

The door opened, he only knew because a fresh cool breeze drafted over his shoulders. Looking up he saw Jax and Dodge enter, both of their faces grave.

"What have they told you?" Dodge asked.

"She's in good hands." His voice croaked out.

Jax sat in the chair next to his, Dodge on the other side of Jax and they waited silently.

After long moments Jax said, "She's super strong. Almost as strong as me."

He looked over at her and she had a grin on her face. He bumped her with his shoulder and shook his head. Taking a deep breath to get his emotions in check he replied, "She's stronger than you are."

They all laughed out loud. But only for a second or two.

The door opened again and the nurse who brought him here entered. "Sir, we need someone who can sign papers on her behalf. She needs to have surgery, but we can't operate without permission.

"We have no one here who can sign for her. One of her brothers lives in Japan and the other one is in the service in South Carolina. Her parents were recently murdered and we have reason to believe that same person shot her." He was beginning to panic.

The nurse nodded and said, "Okay, let me tell the doctors. They can sign for her if they believe it is life threatening."

Life threatening. Oh shit. He jumped up from his chair and began to pace. What in the hell could they do?

46

Opening her eyes, she saw darkness out the window. Blinking a few times, she tried to remember what had happened. Moving her hand to her stomach she felt the tenderness there and remembered being shot.

Moving her head to look around the room she saw Hawk, sleeping in the chair next to her bed. Dodge and Jax were cuddled in the recliner in the room sleeping. Wyatt was sitting in a chair closer to the door, his head back against the wall, his eyes closed in sleep. The only sounds in the room were the soft steady breathing of her friends.

The door opened and Wyatt jumped up and scared the poor nurse who came in to check on her. Her little yelp woke the rest of the room's occupants up. Each of them first looking at Wyatt and the nurse, then at her.

Hawk sprang from his chair and took her hand. "Hey, how are you?"

She looked into his tired eyes and knew two things.

She loved him. She honest to goodness loved him. She had always asked her mom how she'd know if she loved someone and her mom said, "You just will." At the time she thought her mom just didn't want to answer her, but now she knew she was telling the truth. She just knew.

The other thing she knew was he loved her. It was in his eyes. The worry, concern, care and love. When you look deep enough into a person's eyes, you could see their soul. She saw his.

"Well, I have a hole in my stomach that wasn't there this morning and a bunch of people who are supposed to be rehearsing for a wedding sleeping in my room."

Jax laughed. "We don't need to rehearse, we've so got this."

"But, I ruined your rehearsal. I'm so sorry."

Dodge stood next to Jax, his arm around her shoulders. "You didn't ruin anything. Besides, the rehearsal was all Pilar's idea. She wanted tradition." He looked into Jax's eyes and she smiled. "We don't care about any of that."

Jax giggled. "Although, Pilar will be having a word with you I'm afraid."

She dropped her head back. "I think I can handle it. Maybe when your brother gets married, she can get her tradition."

That made the room erupt into laughter and even though she didn't get the joke, she figured she'd find out one day. Right now, she was a bit sleepy.

The nurse came over to the bed and checked her chart. Then asked her to open her mouth for the thermometer, after tucking it under her tongue, the nurse wrapped a blood pressure cuff around her arm and began taking her readings.

Removing the cuff, she said, " Your blood pressure is very good, Roxanne."

She smiled around the thermometer, not like she was actually doing anything to make it good, so, there was that. The thermometer beeped and the nurse looked at the temperature. "You're only slightly above normal, the doctors will be happy with that.

Roxanne grinned, "I happen to think I'm more than slightly above normal, but we can leave it at that."

The nurse giggled and Jax said, "She's going to be fine."

Putting things away, writing on her chart and hanging it at the end of the bed the nurse asked, "Is there anything I can get you? A little water perhaps?"

Clearing her throat, she said, "Water would be amazing."

The nurse turned to the rest of them and said, "It's nearly 9:30, you should let her get some sleep."

Jax walked to the side of the bed and took her hand. "I'm glad you'll be back to normal soon. So sorry we didn't get to you in time. We tried calling and texting, but we couldn't get through. The hotel wouldn't tell us what room you were in, which, of course, they shouldn't. So, we had to wait downstairs. We didn't have time to search downstairs, but we were watching for any signs of that asshole. But we didn't see him till he stepped out of the room. I don't think the hotel would have let us search."

"I don't blame you. Any of you." Finding the remote to the bed with her right hand, she pressed the button to raise her head a bit. "I saw him when I checked in. I thought I did anyway. He stepped off the elevator then when I looked up, he stepped back in. I thought it was Raymond, but logic told me it wasn't. But, I was worried about getting ready and back to the house, so I just put it out of my mind. I should have been more careful."

Wyatt stepped forward, "No one expects to be ambushed and you can't live your life if you're worried it will happen at any moment. Glad you're okay, Roxanne."

"Thanks."

Wyatt walked to the door. "I'll see you guys back at the compound."

He left the room, then Jax squeezed her hand. "We'll be going, too. If they don't spring you from here tomorrow, which is doubtful, we'll stop by and see you after I'm Mrs. Sager." The smile on her face rivaled the sun, simply stunning.

"Sounds good. You two have a good night."

Jax squeezed her hand again and Dodge waved then they left the room.

She took a deep breath and let it out, then turned her head to look at Hawk. The green of his eyes was mesmerizing and ever changing. His thick dark lashes were envy inducing.

"I'm going to hang around tonight, Roxanne." He took her hand in his and perched himself on the edge of the bed.

"Oh, you don't have to, Hawk. You need your rest, too."

"I'll be fine. I've slept in a lot worse places than this. Besides, if anything happened to you, I'd never forgive myself. I'm having a hard time forgiving myself now."

She saw moisture gather in his eyes and remembered his wife, Sarah. "Are you comparing what happened with Sarah to what happened with me?"

His Adam's apple bobbed up and down a few times and she watched him gather his composure. He nodded. "I don't know if I'll ever be able to forgive myself."

She softly asked. "For Sarah or for me?"

"For both of you."

She pulled his hand to her lips and kissed his knuckles. "Hawk, look at me."

Slowly his eyes looked into hers. "We never know when it's our time to go. Ever. Look at what happened to my parents. And there is nothing you can do about a crazed, hateful person going batshit crazy and killing people. But, you did everything you could do and you shot him before he had the chance to shoot me again. So, you did save me."

"But you still got shot."

"Right, and now I'll have a scar to match one of yours. But, I'm not dead, because you saved me. You changed the pattern. You did it, Tiger."

"Tiger? No."

"Yes, I like it and think it's the perfect nickname for you."

"Sweetheart, my nickname is Hawk."

She giggled. "What's your real name?"

He grimaced and went silent. She shook his hand back and forth and he cleared his throat. "You better not tell anyone what my real name is. Only Gaige really knows."

"I can keep a secret."

"Hank."

"What's wrong with Hank?"

"I don't like it. I had a classmate in grade school whose name was Hank and he was a bully."

"You're not a bully." Sad that he associated his name with a bully's name.

"No, but you're still not going to call me Hank."

"Okay. I can live with that." She took a breath. "Hawk, I've been thinking."

He reached forward and placed his forefinger over her lips. "Wait, let me go first."

Her eyebrows rose but she waited. "I love you, Luna. More than I ever dreamed could happen. More than anything." His voice cracked and her heart swelled.

"I love you, too."

47

Hawk wheeled her into the decorated and cleaned foyer and Roxanne sighed when she saw the transformation. The lights had been crisscrossed above sparkled through the gossamer and lent a soft but romantic feel to the room. The Mandevilla had opened their blossoms overnight and created a soft color palette to the room. The white doors and the hard-wood floors created a homey atmosphere. Even he had to admit, it was stunning.

The white chairs had been set up into two sections, creating an aisle in between. The chairs on the ends of each row were decorated with gossamer bows with a trailing tail and a pink Mandevilla tucked into the top.

"Wow, this is just perfect." She said softly.

Hawk went to the hotel to gather her things and brought them all to the hospital so she could wash up and get dressed, while she called her brothers and Carmella and explained what had happened. She wasn't able to take a shower. She fussed and worried about things women worried about. Did she smell bad, she didn't have the strength to do her hair, but Skye had come to the hospital and helped her pull it up. No matter what she wore or how her hair looked, she was gorgeous and he tried reassuring her of that.

"You all did a great job of decorating. Pilar fussed over the flowers most of the night, I'm told."

"She probably wanted to stay busy after having plans change so quickly." She giggled.

He rolled her wheelchair to the end of the front row, not the aisle side, and she whispered, "I shouldn't sit up here."

"Jax insisted. I'm not fighting with her and you're in no condition, so just enjoy it."

He sat next to her and took her hand in his, resting them on the arm of the wheelchair. Dr. Jamison had let her out on a two-hour pass after much begging and complaining. He had given her strict orders to not leave her chair, no alcohol, no lifting, stretching and very little movement. All this after constant begging from Roxanne and the threat that she'd check herself out if he didn't give permission. Since the internal injuries were not life threatening, he conceded but still laid out the strict orders. Then the doctor made him agree to ensure she'd follow orders.

The room filled up, mostly GHOST employees and their wives. Jax's mother, Pilar, and, of course, her twin, Josh, as well as Dodge's parents and his two brothers were there. He looked back just as Gaige's sister, Keirnan and her husband, Dane walked in and he nodded and waved. It had been years since he'd seen them. He'd make it a point to catch up with them before he took Roxanne back to the hospital.

The music began to play, Making Memories of Us the

chosen song, and Pilar huffed. Hawk chuckled and so did Roxanne next to him, poor Pilar fussed and fussed that weddings should remain traditional, but her little girl was anything but traditional. Jax and Dodge stayed true to themselves through everything, and he admired that.

The men walked out from the kitchen and stood to the right of the altar, Dodge first, then Ford, then Lincoln. The altar was a table in front of them with a Bible on a stand and two large candles. Three smaller candles were arranged between the large candles, all of them pink in color and unlit.

Megan walked down the aisle wearing a long white dress with beading on the top, her auburn hair piled on her head. Roxanne whispered to him, "She's beautiful."

Looking into her eyes he saw her sincerity, the awe in what she was witnessing and how tired she looked. He kissed her nose and held her hand tighter and she smiled at him. His heartbeat sped up. No doubt about it, she had a hold on him. "She is."

Skye walked down next, her blond hair arranged the same as Megan's, same white dress, same comment from Roxanne.

The music grew louder and everyone rose. Hawk stood and moved Roxanne's chair toward the front and to the side so she could see Jax walk down the aisle.

In true Jax fashion, the little beauty appeared at the end of the aisle, her brother Josh escorting her. He wore a pink tie to match her pink dress. Her dark hair was pulled back, but curled instead of in a ponytail or braid as it usually was, and she had pink flowers tucked here and there inside the curls. No veil, the long full flowing dress was the only ornamentation besides the flowers and she wore it beautifully.

Turning his head to see Dodge's reaction was probably better than seeing Jax in a dress for the first time. His smile broadened as he looked at her, then his eyes teared up. Swiping at them with his thumb, then saw Dodge laugh and looked at Jax to see her lift her dress and she was wearing her Army style everyday boots underneath. She winked at him and his admiration grew for her again. Keeping it real. That was Jax.

He heard Roxanne giggle and he bent down and kissed the top of her head. She whispered, "I just love her spirit."

"Yep, she has it in spades."

Jax walked down the aisle, met Dodge and watched as Josh shook his hand. Dodge turned to look at her but she held up a forefinger to wait, turned and walked to Roxanne, bent down and kissed her cheek. "Thanks for coming, Luna. I heard you had to fight with the doctor for permission. You got spunk. I think I have a girl crush."

Looking at him then, she smiled and said, "You got your hands full buddy and you deserve it."

She winked at Roxanne and bounced back to Dodge who was nodding and smiling at his spunky bride.

The folks gathered together sat and he moved Roxanne back to their position, sat alongside her and took her hand in his again. That's when he knew what he had to do.

48

The wedding was pure Jax and Dodge and incredibly enjoyable. Not only was she a beautiful bride, her spunk and sass showed through and Dodge looked completely and utterly smitten. It was perfect.

They walked back down the aisle to the song by Darius Rucker, History in the Making and just like the first song, this one was perfect for them as well. She stifled a sigh. Must be the meds.

Hawk turned to look at her. "How are you feeling? We've got forty-five minutes before you have to go, so tell me who you want to chat with and save me at least fifteen minutes to introduce you to Gaige's sister, Keirnan and her husband, Dane. She's the reason GHOST came to be."

"Oh, I'd love to hear that story."

"How about on the way back to the hospital?"

"Deal. I'd like to just have a moment to congratulate Jax and Dodge and say hello to the other women, Megan, Skye and Sophie if you don't mind."

He brushed her cheek with the back of his fingers.

"You're warm, are you sure you can manage forty-five minutes?"

"I'm fine. I have to miss so much, at least give me this time."

He leaned forward and kissed her lips softly and she practically swooned. Meds and wedding atmosphere - a deadly combination.

He stood and began pushing her toward the people gathered at the back of the foyer close to the office door. Megan quickly came to her, leaned down and hugged her shoulders. "How are you feeling, Roxanne?"

"I'm good, just tired. And you look amazing."

"Thank you. Are you over-exerting yourself? You feel warm. Remember, I'm a nurse so don't lie to me."

"It's a lot, I won't lie, but I just couldn't come all this way and miss this."

Megan patted her shoulder and moved over as Skye approached.

"Oh, I'm so happy you were released to join us." Skye bent and hugged Roxanne. "Wasn't it the best?"

" Absolutely. You are stunning in that dress."

"Thank you. You look amazing, Roxanne. After all you've been through, I'm in awe."

She giggled, "Thank my hairstylist."

Sophie and Gaige came next and were so kind. Before long she'd spoken to each of the GHOST team, except Jax and Dodge, who were still busy chatting with guests. Pilar came over to her and shook hands with her, holding her hand instead of releasing it, and placing her other hand over the top. "My dear, I am so sorry for your troubles. I'm praying you'll be right as rain in no time. And, since you have a handsome protector, you should be safe as they come."

"Thank you, Mrs. Masters."

"No, Pilar. In case you haven't noticed, this is not a formal affair." Pilar bent down close to her ear. "That girl has always had a mind of her own. Dodge, he has his hands full."

She laughed since that was exactly what Jax had said to Hawk. She looked back at him and he was grinning from ear to ear.

"Mama, I hope you aren't complaining about my shoes to Roxanne. You should have seen what she was wearing the first time I met her." Jax teased.

Her cheeks burned bright as she remembered her old hipster jeans and fringed midriff baring top. "Gosh, don't remind me."

Jax kneeled in front of her. "Seriously, how are you doing?"

"I'm tired. I'm also happy as can be for you and Dodge. Thrilled to be alive and feeling positive about the future."

"Perfect. That's all good news."

"Tell me about the boots. What on earth possessed you?"

Jax laughed. "Mama was fussing about shoes on the phone a couple of weeks ago and what I'd be wearing and I said my work boots. She had a fit. After the call Dodge told me, and I quote, "You don't have the balls to wear those for the wedding." You know me - game on."

She laughed and a sharp pain sliced through her stomach. Wrapping her arm around her waist her breath caught.

"Easy on her, Jax." Hawk admonished from behind her. He stepped alongside and knelt. "Hey, we should go now, you're getting tired and..." He felt her forehead and cheeks. "You're burning up."

Catching her breath, she said, "No, you wanted to talk to Keirnan and Dane."

"I can do it later."

"Please, just a few more minutes. I promise not to laugh." Turning to Jax she winked. The smile Jax bestowed on her was brilliant. She leaned up and kissed her cheek, then stood and said, "Don't be too long and I'll come and see you later."

"By later I hope you mean tomorrow, this is your wedding night."

Jax laughed as Dodge came over and put his arm around her shoulders. "Roxanne, I see you're still making my wife laugh."

"She does the same to me."

Keirnan and Dane walked over to them then and Hawk stood and hugged Keirnan and shook Dane's hand. "You two look amazing and I hear you have three kids now."

She watched his face change from the worry a moment ago, to genuine happiness and friendliness as he spoke to his longtime friends. He introduced her to them, and she could see the resemblance in Keirnan's eyes to Gaige's.

They generally chatted about catching up and Keirnan bent down and said, "Gaige told me what happened. I'm so sorry for what you're going through, but I also hear you're strong, stay that way and next time we visit, which is next month for my brother's wedding, I'll expect to see you walking around and laughing heartily."

"Deal."

Hawk raised his voice a bit and said, "We're leaving now, you all keep the noise to a minimum."

He walked behind her and began pushing her chair to

the elevator to well wishes from the wedding guests. She smiled and waved her goodbyes, but gads she was tired.

They took the elevator to the garage and once at the truck, Hawk leaned down and lifted her easily, careful to not jostle her, and set her in the seat. She managed her seatbelt as he placed the hospital wheelchair in the back. It took more energy that she would have dreamed.

Holding the seatbelt away from her bandages with her left hand, she prepared for the ride back to the hospital. Hitting even the slightest bumps and dips in the road caused more pain than she'd admit to anyone.

49

"Ready?"

"Yes."

He pulled the truck from its parking place and drove smoothly up and out of the underground garage. Navigating the driveway was a breeze, navigating the roads was harder. He fought between keeping speed even and watching the road's patterns to minimize bumps and jostling and quickly getting Roxanne back to the hospital. Her color was eerily pale.

Deciding to keep her mind occupied, he said, "So Keirnan and Dane's story, it's rather amazing."

A brief glance at Roxanne had him halting his story. She had fallen asleep.

Driving quietly back to the hospital his mind was whirling in so many directions it was dizzying. He'd held himself away from personal entanglements for so long because of Sarah and his fear of losing someone he loved again. And call him crazy and maybe caught up a bit in the whole wedding mania, but he longed for what his friends had found. And, Jax, that little vixen, had said to him just after she spoke to Roxanne, "Hawk, you've just been given a gift in Roxanne. Don't be a regifter."

He pulled into the hospital parking lot, quietly stepped from the vehicle, looking at each vehicle, each person walking in or out, for signs of anything at all nefarious. Gaige still hadn't gotten information back on the man he shot yesterday and whether he had any travel companions with him initially. Evil lurked everywhere.

Pulling the wheelchair from the back, he opened it and wheeled it around to the passenger door. Glancing in to make sure Roxanne wasn't leaning against it, he opened it slowly and reached in to unbuckle her seatbelt. Holding her right hand out of the way as he released it, he whispered in her ear. "Luna, we're here."

Her eyes opened and stared ahead for a few beats as she seemed to be disoriented. Blinking her eyes then landed on his. Smiling he said, "I'm going to lift you out of the truck and set you in your chair. Ready?"

She nodded without saying a thing. When he lifted her, she moaned slightly and sweat formed on his forehead. He didn't want to cause her any pain. A nurse came from inside and took control of the wheelchair. "I'll get her upstairs for you."

A valet came and handed him a ticket with a red number written on it, hopped in his truck and drove away.

He walked behind the nurse quietly. His brain needed a break.

≈

"Should we come back later?"

His eyes flew open as he heard Sophie's voice. At the foot of Roxanne's bed stood Gaige and Sophie, hand in hand, staring at him. Gaige grinned at him, pointed to his hand, which lay on the bed holding Roxanne's hand. He sat up in the recliner he'd been dozing in, the blanket someone tossed over him fell into his lap as he looked at it and wondered when he'd been covered up.

"Hi. You been staring long?"

Gaige laughed. "No, we just got here. We thought we'd stop by and update you with the intel that came in about an hour ago."

He looked at Roxanne, peacefully sleeping. Relieved to see her color had returned he refused to remove his hand from hers. Motioning with his head, "You two take a seat. Thanks for coming, I've been worrying about what comes next."

Sophie smiled. "Seems so."

"Shut up." He quipped.

Sophie giggled and Roxanne said, "Hi."

Slowly adjusting herself in bed, she reached for the remote, which laid next to her right hand, and raised herself up.

Gaige nodded. "The intel we received is complete. Roxanne's shooter," his eyes bounced to Roxanne, "was the same man who shot the Bowmans and the Prime Minister. He shot them via drone, just as Roxanne suspected. The drone was found in his room. The gun attached to it was taken in for ballistics testing and the bullets matched those at the State Department's DS's evidence room. He also acted alone here on US soil. Of course, he had assistance back home."

Roxanne breathed in and slowly out. "He was the one. He was the man following my mom before he killed her."

"Yes. It appears he had some surgery done about six

months ago, to make him appear more like Raymond so your mom wouldn't be afraid. Even though she mentioned seeing him to you, Roxanne, we don't have another person who has said that she mentioned him to them. Including the friend she met for coffee each week. So, we can only guess that she chalked it up to Raymond being mentally unwell or his usual, but odd, behavior. If she mentioned anything to your father, we don't have evidence of it."

Roxanne's voice was soft. "Okay. She didn't seem scared when she mentioned it to me, just more perplexed than anything."

Gaige continued. "Right. That seemed to be the plan. This man, his name is..."

Roxanne's voice raised. "No, I don't want to know it. He's evil and someone I don't care to humanize."

"Fair enough." Gaige responded. "He's from the Azerbaitani Prosperity Party. The Prime Minister was not the actual target, your father was. The information your dad was gathering on them was astronomical. And, would bring that party down, which I'm happy to say, it has done. Our President is speaking with the existing party in power in Azerbaitani and relaying the information our government , Leland and Raymond gathered; so far, many of the top members of the Prosperity Party have been arrested and taken into custody . It's little consolation Roxanne, but your father's ultimate goal is being realized, at great cost I'm afraid."

Turning to look at Roxanne, he was relieved to see she wasn't going to break down crying. She squeezed his hand then responded, "He'd have said to me that sometimes great cost comes with great reward. He never shirked his duties to his country. And in this instance, it was keeping [our government from funding] the Azerbaitani government expansion only for this evil party, which took many opposition lives, to take over on our dime and create massive chaos. The Prosperity Party wants an all-out World War."

Standing he stretched his back, walked to Gaige and shook his hand. "Thanks for bringing this information to us, Gaige." Looking back at Roxanne, he smiled, "We'll both rest easier now."

50

Slipping her arms into her long-sleeved, light blue t-shirt, the nurse helped her pull it down in the back. She'd had a bit of a setback after leaving for the wedding for her two hours, but the doctor refrained from saying, "I told you so." She'd been in the hospital for close to four days now and she was eager to get out of here.

Still sitting on the edge of her bed, she tugged her drawstring, loose-fitting pants over her legs, and held on as she slowly stepped down to the floor. Pulling her pants up to her waist she smiled, she did it and she wasn't exhausted afterwards. Progress.

A knocking sounded on the door and the nurse looked at her, "Ready?"

Tugging her t-shirt over the top of her pants, she said, "Yes."

The nurse pulled the curtain back to the wall, exposing the entire room and she said, "Come in."

Hawk, looking fresh, clean and incredibly handsome entered the room. He stood straight and tall and her knees actually wobbled, but this time it wasn't because she was weak or tired, he was just that damned sexy.

"Good morning. You look fantastic, Roxanne." He walked directly to her, and gently wrapped his arms around her. The aroma of his aftershave and shower soap, which was part of the whole of this man, enveloped her and felt just so right. They'd spent so much time together these past few days, talking, poking jokes at each other, his friends included as they came to visit her. Hawk was always present and at her side. This morning he told her he needed to check in at the house and grab a shower and he'd be here at 10:00 to pick her up. Punctual to a fault, here he was at exactly 10:00.

"So, do you." She sighed into his chest. Her arms wrapped around his waist and she enjoyed the feel of him all over again.

"I have everything set for you at the house. You'll get a key card so you can get into the house from the garage, you'll have access to anything you need, and Mrs. James and Kylie are cooking up a storm for the team members who are not on a mission right now. Wyatt, Axel and Josh are gone. But we'll eat together, and you can rest when you need to."

"Hawk, I'll have to go home soon. I do have a job; the firm has been very understanding of my absence, but they won't be understanding forever."

"I know and we'll talk about that soon."

The nurse fussed with packing up Roxanne's things, the 'courtesy plastic cup, vomit pan, hand lotion and toiletries' she'd been given, and brought a cart up to carry all the flowers she'd been sent while there. Gorgeous arrangements from her brothers and their families, her office and the GHOST crew. Her room smelled like a funeral home; she had spent far too much time in recently and she complained of it to Hawk just yesterday. He chuckled and said he agreed.

Another nurse came in with a wheelchair and when her shoulders slumped the nurse apologetically said, "Sorry hun, hospital policy."

Hawk patted her ass and teased, "Get in your chariot, Luna."

She sat without assistance, proud of herself all over again and the second nurse began wheeling her as the other followed with her bag of goodies and Hawk manned the flower cart.

The ride back to GHOST was enjoyable. Much more than the last time. Her pain had lessened quite a bit, she wasn't completely exhausted, and she felt apprehensive but still so hopeful. Mulling around in her mind how to bring up the distance that would soon be between them, she was irritated with herself that the right words still hadn't come to her.

The sun shone through the windows, soft music played on the radio and Hawk held her hand. That was a pretty good beginning to the day, and she didn't want to mar it by worrying about leaving.

He pulled into the garage at GHOST and she waited as he walked around to the passenger side to open her door. It was nice having him treat her like a lady and it didn't bother her in the least that he wanted to. Opening her door, she smiled at his handsome face as his eyes landed on her. He leaned in and kissed her lips, softly but oh so sweetly. "Do you need help getting down?"

"No." She giggled and hoped that was true, but she wanted to do this.

Holding the grab handle mounted inside his truck

along the windshield, she held herself steady as she stepped down. Not bad.

Stepping into the elevator, he swiped his card and they rode up to the second floor. The house was quiet as they walked along the hall upstairs, the foyer once again transformed to the neat and clean entry area, all visible signs of the wedding gone. It was still beautiful, but a bit sad that it was all over. Hawk waived his card and opened his bedroom door, and let her step in before him.

She walked into the room, inhaled deeply of the scent of Hawk and closed her eyes a moment to enjoy it.

"Sit down and relax and I'll get your things from the truck. She laughed, "Hawk, don't fuss."

He closed the door, held up his hands and admitted. "I'm nervous."

"What? You? Big badass tiger?"

"Stop it."

Laughing again she sat on the sofa, the soft leather felt great. "Why are you nervous, Hawk?"

He came and sat next to her, taking her hand in his, but twisted to the side so he looked at her. "Roxanne, we haven't talked about the future."

She took a deep breath. "No. We haven't."

"I want to."

"Okay. I do, too."

He scooted forward, "I'd like to go first." He dropped to one knee, pulled a shiny object from his pocket and held it up to her. "Will you marry me?"

She stared at the ring in his fingers, glinting in the sunlight streaming in through the tall windows across the room, speechless.

He continued. "We've known each other only a short amount of time. But, I know for a fact that I want to spend the rest of my days with you. I love you, Luna. My heart finally feels whole again because of you."

The shiny ring in his fingers floated through the tears in her eyes. His eyes so earnest and beautiful stared into hers, waiting for her answer. Without any doubts in her mind she said, "I absolutely will marry you."

"For real?"

She giggled as tears tracked down her cheeks. "For real, Tiger."

His fingers shook as he placed the ring on her finger, then held her hand to his heart, his over the top. "I love you with my whole heart, Luna."

Leaning forward, her right hand snaked around his nape and pulled his lips to hers. Kissing him with all she had, trying to convey everything she felt in this moment. Pulling away she said, "I love you to, Hawk. With my whole heart."

51

Her phone rang and he turned to see if she heard it.

Snagging it from the nightstand she looked at the screen, smiled a cheesy 'hope this is a good news smile' and answered. "Roxanne Bowman."

He watched her as she stood across her bedroom in Chesterton, the suitcase opened half-filled and packing boxes all around. Her posture was straight, her figure lean and her mane of long white-blond hair was pulled together at her nape and trailing down her back.

"Okay, thank you very much, I'm looking forward to it. See you a week from tomorrow."

Tapping the end call icon, she ran to him, jumped up into his arms and squeezed his neck tightly. "I got the job."

"I had no doubt." He kissed her lips, this amazing woman who would soon be his wife, and marveled at their path to this place here and now. She'd quit her job in Washington two months ago and stayed with him at GHOST as she healed and they enjoyed getting to know each other. Now they were currently packing up her apartment which was a ninety minute drive from her childhood home.

"I can't wait to get back now. I'm so excited."

"More excited about the job than the wedding?"

She pulled back and looked into his eyes as he set her down. "Of course, I am, can't you tell?"

He laughed then, she was constantly teasing him.

"So, this law firm you'll be working at, they'll let you work from home?"

"Yes, they've agreed that I only have to come in once a week to have face to face time. It'll be perfect."

She turned and continued to pack up her nightstand and he continued to pull books from a bookshelf in her bedroom. Her phone rang again but he continued packing. He was ridiculously eager to get Roxanne home, their home, at GHOST, and out of Washington. Mostly, their wedding was coming soon, neither of them wanted to wait long, and he was crazily excited. Who would have thought?

"Oh no, really?"

Uh oh, that didn't sound good and her tone turned instantly sad. "Of course, I understand, I just never dreamed I'd marry and you wouldn't be there."

Yesterday, Matthew had called her and said he wasn't able to get back in time for the wedding, but he and his family would be back in the US around Christmas and they'd spend time together then. Since they lived in Japan, and he and Roxanne weren't giving folks a lot of time to plan, it was understandable.

Stepping from the closet she dropped her phone on the bed and flopped down next to it. "Now, Brendan can't come. I won't have any family at our wedding. Well, Carmella will be there, but it's not the same."

"Neither will I, but we have each other."

He was quiet for a moment, then inhaled deeply and said, "Call me crazy but..."

He knelt in front of her, swept her hands up into his and said, "Why don't we get married today?"

She giggled. Staring into his eyes, he saw it. The moment she realized he was serious. He pressed on. "Look, Jax and Dodge just got married at the compound. Gaige and Sophie are, too. We don't need to be like them, we'll do our own thing, elope, then at Christmas when Matthew and his family are at Lynyrd Station we'll have a party. Maybe that will give Brendan enough time to make plans to be there and we'll all celebrate together."

Her hands framed his face, her thumbs smoothing his cheeks as she stared at him. "It makes total sense. And, I love the idea of being different. And, of course, I love you and it really only matters what we want."

Smiling at her, he replied. "Exactly." Letting her muse on this was necessary.

"I have a silver dress in the closet I can wear. I have matching shoes, too."

She kissed his lips then continued. "It takes about two to three hours to get the marriage license all prepared, so we could get rings and flowers in that time and then go back to the courthouse to get married."

His smile grew. "I love the way you think."

Her smile was brilliant when she replied, "I love the idea. Let's do it."

Kissing her lips, he pushed her back on the bed, his lips never leaving hers, until he lay over her slender body. Her legs instantly wrapped around his waist, so he pushed against her a few times until she began wriggling under him. Reaching between them, he tugged on her yoga pants, once again praising the inventor, and when he met with resistance, she arched her back, making it easier for him to pull them down, exposing the parts he wanted at this moment.

Kissing her chin, and down her throat to under her ear, she moaned softly and raised her hips to create more friction. Her hands reached between them and unbuttoned his jeans, as she slid the zipper down releasing him, he groaned at the freedom he felt. She tucked her toes into the waistband of his jeans and pushed them down his legs with hers. It was a little trick she'd shown him a couple months ago and it was one of his favorites.

His jeans around his knees, his thickened length lay on her and he rolled his hips, enticing her more. Her hand again reached between them, wrapped around his penis and slowly rubbed him up, then down, then up, on and on, until he felt the pre-cum drip from him. They were a finely tuned clock because she could sense his readiness; she positioned him at her entrance, lifted her hips and his head pushed inside her. Needing no more coaxing, he thrust his hips and she let out a slow, soft moan as he began moving inside of her. Their hips met and separated, as they enjoyed this mating dance, each beginning to sweat, but enjoying their lovemaking far too much to care.

Her breathing increased and her legs tightened and he knew she was close. Rolling his hips a few more times, she mewled as her release erupted around him and he held still for just a moment to enjoy the look on her face as she reached her orgasm. Best. Look. Ever.

When her orgasm had subsided, he began pumping into her, eager for his own. Her hands grabbed his butt cheeks and urged him on, until he exploded into her. Needing a breather, he held himself over her, so he didn't crush her, and her hands splayed on his back, under his t-shirt, which he hadn't even taken the time to remove. Her top was still on as well, so they were even.

Once he'd caught his breath, he kissed her lips, and trailed kisses to her ear where he whispered, "Let's clean up and get married."

Driving to the courthouse, he found Judge Martin Dishman's office he'd called while he waited for Roxanne to shower and change. Judge Dishman agreed to officiate the ceremony. He held the door for Roxanne, and stood at the desk as his Assistant finished a telephone call.

"How can I help you?"

"My name is Hawk Delaney; this is my fiancée' Roxanne Bowman and Judge Dishman has agreed to marry us this afternoon."

He reached over and took Roxanne's hand in his and she squeezed.

"Absolutely. I'm Angie, the Judge's Assistant. You need to go down to the clerk's office on the first floor and get your license, and then when it's ready come back to this office. Do you have any witnesses?"

Roxanne smiled sweetly and said, "We don't. Would you be our witness?"

Angie looked truly honored and replied, "I'd love to. Thank you."

"We'll be back in a few hours."

Wrapping his arm around Roxanne's shoulders, he directed them to the door. Making their way to the clerk's office his heart was full. It had been a long time, so long, since he'd felt completely whole. The trouble was, he didn't even know he wasn't whole until he met Roxanne. Life was weird.

Walking into the clerk's office he was relieved to see

only two people in the longest line of four windows, so it shouldn't take long. Waiting their turn, they stood, arms around each other's waist, and far too many men looking at Roxanne. She was simply stunning in her silver dress. Sleek and long it flowed down her body like water and made her long white mane look stunning. She'd curled her hair and let it hang over her shoulders, mingling with the beaded top. She sparkled on her own, without the dress, but in the dress, she simply glowed.

At the window they presented their driver's licenses, and a second form of ID; he paid for the license and they were told to come back in two hours. It felt like eternity, but they had a few things to do.

52

She kept tearing up as they managed each of their tasks. She'd put getting married from her mind long ago. Now here she was, getting married in her own way especially for a Bowman. This was their own way and it felt good. She imagined Jax would be pissy at not being here, but she'd get over it and they'd celebrate in December.

She held the tiny box with their wedding rings in her hand, the jeweler had been easy to deal with and found the perfect wedding band for her to match the sparkling solitaire Hawk had given her when he proposed. Her band was wide, glittered with diamonds, and hard to miss. That had been at Hawk's insistence. "You don't leave the house without this on your finger. You're off the market."

"As are you, Tiger." His band was black tungsten. Solid, strong and dark, just like him.

He smiled, but she knew there was still maybe some insecurity on his part; this was so new to both of them and the past two months they'd been holed up at GHOST, ignoring the rest of the world. Soon they'd both be out and about, working and spending, hopefully short amounts of time away from each other, and they both needed the reassurances. One thing she knew without a doubt, she loved Hawk with her whole heart, and she felt his love in return.

He stopped in front of a flower shop. "Stay here, let me run in and pick the perfect flowers for you."

She smiled, "You are forever surprising me, Hawk."

He winked and jumped out of the truck, closing the door he motioned to her to press the lock button.

She did as he asked and watched his fine ass stroll in front of the truck and into the flower shop. He wasn't in there long, before she heard a commotion, yelling and swearing and damned if it didn't sound like Hawk. Soon the door to the flower shop flew open and out tumbled a scrawny looking kid, couldn't have been more than seventeen or eighteen years old, tattered clothes and a dirty face.

Hawk stepped out behind him, lifted him by the front of his dark blue hoodie, got nose to nose with him, said something to him; the kid's head bobbed up and down, then Hawk shoved him away. The kid stumbled back, caught himself and took off running.

Hawk glanced at her, smirked, then stepped back inside and emerged a second later with a gorgeous bouquet of blush pink roses, deep purple lilies and silvery dusty miller tucked in here and there. It was stunning. She unlocked the truck as he neared, then stared as he pulled himself into the truck and handed her the bouquet, the sweetest smile on his face.

"These are stunning," she said, just before smelling the fragrant flowers.

"She whipped them up for you, just before that stupid kid pulled his stunt."

"Do tell, what was that stunt?"

Chuckling, "He had his finger in his hoodie pocket, pretending to be a gun and tried robbing the store."

"Hawk to the rescue," she mused.

He grinned. "It's really all in a day's work, Luna."

Glancing at her, the look in his eyes said everything she needed to know right now. He loved her, it was right there. She smiled at him and he said, "Let's go get married."

Nodding she clutched her flowers in one hand and their rings in the other and her heartbeat raced. They were getting married.

Walking into the courthouse with their purchases, she felt giddy as passersby stared, smiled and took a second look. Of course, they could have been looking at the badass walking beside her. He had deep gray dress pants on and a black button up shirt, the sleeves rolled to below his elbow. The myriad of tattoos on his arms were visible which in dress clothes were such a contrast and yet so darned yummy.

He held the door open for her, his smile so sexy, and she brushed against him as she entered the courthouse. He swatted her butt and whispered, "All night long, Luna."

The shiver that skittered down her spine excited her. Entering the office of Judge Dishman, Angie greeted them with a big smile. "There you are, I just got a call from the clerk and she's bringing your marriage license up right now."

Hawk grinned. "Now that's service, I expected I'd have to go down to get it. We just wanted you to know we were here in the courthouse."

"Maggie, the head clerk, is a friend of mine and I called her after you left and asked if she could work on that one personally."

When things like this happened, she knew it was meant to be. "Thank you so much."

Angie looked directly at her. "Ms. Bowman, Judge Dishman knew your father, they golfed together, and he wanted to make sure you had the best experience you could have. We're both very sorry for your loss."

Blinking rapidly to keep from spilling tears, she smiled, but couldn't say anything just then. She'd tried hard all day not to cry about the fact that she was getting married and her parents weren't here to witness it. It was her mom's dream for her to find that special someone and join together with him.

The clerk entered the door, saving her from embarrassment. "Looks like I'm just in time." She smiled broadly at her accomplishment.

Sending a silent prayer and hello to her parents, something told her they were here, and she knew in spirit they'd always be with her.

Angie led them to Judge Dishman's Chambers where he waited wearing his black robe and greeted them all with a smile. "Hello and congratulations, Hawk and Roxanne."

He shook hands with Hawk, then with her, and continued to hold her hand as he said. "Your father was a friend and golf buddy of mine and I miss him terribly. I'm sorry for your loss."

Nodding, she swallowed again, took a deep breath and whispered, "Thank you."

Hawk's arm wrapped around her shoulders and the Judge said, "We have a private little grassy area out back, for employees to lunch or take a break; it's the prettiest little spot in the city. How about we go down there and say your vows?"

"Oh, that would be lovely." Looking up at Hawk, his face beamed with happiness.

He nodded, "It would be very nice. Thank you, your Honor."

Judge Dishman led the way and they chatted about light topics as they entered the elevator and rode it down to the lower level. Stepping off into a room, surrounded on three sides with glass, the bright afternoon sun shining in brightened everything up.

The Judge opened the door for them, he and Angie then led them to a small fountain in the corner, against the building. He opened the bible he'd been carrying, lay a sheet of paper on top of it, and began the ceremony.

In just fifteen minutes, they were married, signed the necessary papers, Angie snapped pictures with Hawk's phone and they left the courthouse as Mr. And Mrs. Hank Delany and she was ecstatic.

SNEAK PEEK

The End of Defending Roxanne, GHOST Book Two.

Get book #3, Defending Yvette now.

Continue reading for a Sneak Peek at Defending Yvette, GHOST Book Three, the next novel in the GHOST Series.

DEFENDING YVETTE

CHAPTER 1

Tapping on the picture of her high school friend, Jax, Yvette hit the speaker icon on her phone and tossed it on the bed. She continued hurriedly to throw her clothing into a suitcase as the phone rang on the other end.

"Jax Mas...Sager."

A small giggle sounded after Jax said her name.

"Still not used to your new name?"

"Yvette, how are you?"

Pausing from her packing she swallowed. "I'm in trouble, Jax and I don't know what to do."

"Is that asshole hitting you now?"

Blinking rapidly to stave off the tears, "That's not the whole of it and I have to get out of town."

"Okay, come here to Indiana and tell me what's going on. You can stay with Dodge and I."

Relief flooded through her and she sat on the edge of the bed, and picked up her phone. "Jax, normally I'd say I don't want to be an imposition, but he's going to kill me. As in literally. I found out what he's into and I'm not safe."

"Have you called the police?"

"They won't keep me safe. One of his good buddies works for the local PD and is just as dirty as he is."

"I hate dirty cops. Do you have the means to get here?"

"Yes."

"Okay, keep me posted on your arrival time. I'm on a mission but I'm only one state away and we're leaving in about an hour, so I should be home before you can get there from Florida."

"Thanks, Jax. Really."

"See ya. Stay safe."

The line went dead, typical Jax. She was never overly sentimental. She also didn't understand what it was like to feel as if you couldn't protect yourself. She'd always been so self-assured and able to kick anyone's ass. That's what she was going to have Jax help her with, protecting herself, before it was too late.

She heard a car door slam and peeked out the window, making sure to stay hidden. This was the first time she was happy she lived on the third floor. Not seeing anyone, she continued to fill her suitcase with the things she felt she'd need.

A quick trip to the bathroom for her toothbrush, body wash and a few necessities, she dropped them in a toiletry bag and tossed that into the suitcase as she walked past for one more trip to her closet.

Her stomach was beginning to turn sour the longer she was in her apartment. A couple pair of jogging pants, a few tanks and t-shirts and she was ready to close it up and get the hell out of here.

A text sounded on her phone and a quick glance told her that her flight was on time. She'd booked it before she called Jax, it was the safest place she could think to go.

Zipping her suitcase closed, she slid it down the side of the bed, and pulled the long handle up from the back. Wheeling it down the short hallway to the main living area, she glanced at the clock on the stove. It had been an hour since Randy had threatened her with bodily harm. Actually, mortal force. Normally he'd just say, "Keep your fucking mouth shut or I'll shut it." This time he'd said, "The second I find you; I'll kill you, you lying little snitch." She knew he wasn't lying; she'd gotten in deep this time. Luckily for her, he was out of town, but not sure how far away and how much time she had, she needed to go now.

A quick glance out of the living room window to her vehicle showed no one walking around, nothing out of place. Swallowing nothing but no time to wet her throat, she grabbed her purse from the table by the door, slung it over her shoulder, snatched her suitcase and stepped out of her apartment. She'd figure out what to do with the apartment once she knew whether she could come back and get her things from it. Sliding the key in the deadbolt, she twisted the lock and started her trek to the elevator. Debating on using it or lugging her suitcase down three flights of stairs, she decided on the elevator. Her feet felt like lead as she didn't think she was making time, each passing second felt like an hour.

Finally reaching the elevator, she steered her suitcase into the metal box, jabbed at the down button, and prayed it would close before someone else got on. Swallowing rapidly, she took a deep breath and tried to quell the nausea that sat like acid in her stomach.

The elevator door opened, a car door slammed, and she jumped. She forced down the bile rising from her stomach, took deep breaths and let them out slowly, and tried in vain to stay calm. Nothing could trip her up now, she didn't have the time.

The heat was oppressive and sweat began to trickle down her back. Her hands grew wet and the handle on her suitcase became slippery.

In about three seconds she would burst into tears. Telling herself to hold it together, she repeated this mantra in her head. "I can do this. Be like Jax. I can do this. Be like Jax."

A noise sounded behind her and she turned to see absolutely nothing. She muttered, "I must be losing my mind. Better than my life, I guess."

Looking in both directions for anything unusual, she made a beeline for her car, her pace quickened, the grip on her suitcase iron clad. The sidewalk seemed unusually uneven as she picked up her pace to get to her car. Spotting it only two cars away, she stifled a sob. Nearly running, she was almost there, the sweat now trickling down the side of her face, her vision blurred.

Something jumped on the back of her leg and she fell forward, tumbling over her suitcase and sprawling half on the sidewalk and half on the parking lot. The pavement was scorching hot and she felt her skin burning. Then her stomach twisted when she heard the male voice behind her.

"There you are, you little bitch."

T his concludes your Sneak Peek of Defending Yvette, GHOST Book Three. Grab your copy now to continue reading about Wyatt and Yvette.

Available at www.PJFiala.com

GET MORE DEFENDING YVETTE

T his concludes your Sneak Peek at Defending Roxanne, GHOST Book Two. Grab your copy now to continue reading about Wyatt and Yvette.

Available at www.PJFiala.com/books/DR-Amazon

ENJOY THIS BOOK? YOU CAN MAKE A BIG DIFFERENCE

Reviews are the most powerful tools in my arsenal when it comes to getting attention for my books. As much as I'd like to, I don't have the financial muscle of a New York publisher. I can't take out full page ads in the newspaper or put posters on the subway.

(Not yet, anyway.)

But I do have something much more powerful and effective than that, and it's something that those big publishers would die to get their hands on.

A committed and loyal bunch of readers.

Honest reviews of my books help bring them to the attention of other readers.

If you've enjoyed this book I would be so grateful to you if you could spend just five minutes leaving a review (it can be as short as you like) on the book's vendor page. You can jump right to the page of your choice by clicking below.

Thank you so very much.

ALSO BY PJ FIALA

Click here to see a list of all of my books with the blurbs.

Contemporary Romance

Rolling Thunder Series

Moving to Love, Book 1

Moving to Hope, Book 2

Moving to Forever, Book 3

Moving to Desire, Book 4

Moving to You, Book 5

Moving Home, Book 6

Second Chances Series

Designing Samantha's Love, Book 1

Securing Kiera's Love, Book 2

Military Romantic Suspense

Bluegrass Security Series

Heart Thief, Book One

Finish Line, Book Two

Lethal Love, Book Three

The Bounty Hunters

Ford, Bounty Hunters Book One

Lincoln, Bounty Hunters Book Two

Dodge , Bounty Hunters Book Three

GHOST

GET TWO MORE EBOOKS - FREE!

Building a relationship with my readers is the very best thing about writing. I send monthly newsletters with details on new releases, special offers and other fun things relating to my books or prizes surrounding them.

If you sign up to my mailing list I'll send you all these books for free:

1. A copy of Moving to Love, Book 21 of the Rolling Thunder series.

2. A copy of Moving to Hope, Book 2 of the Rolling Thunder series.

3. A book list so you know what order to read my books in.

You can get the two novels **for free**, by signing up at https://www.subscribepage.com/PJsReadersClub

MEET PJ

PJ is the author of the exciting Rolling Thunder series, Bounty Hunters, Second Chances, Bluegrass Security and the thrilling GHOST series, which is exciting readers with page turning military alphas and the women who love them.

Her online home is https://www.pjfiala.com.
You can connect with her on Facebook at https://www.facebook.com/PJFialaɪ,
on Twitter at @pfiala and
Instagram at https://www.Instagram.com/PJFiala.
If you prefer to email, go ahead, she'll respond -
pjfiala@pjfiala.com.

facebook.com/PJFialaɪ

twitter.com/pfiala

pinterest.com/pattifiala

CPSIA information can be obtained
at www.ICGtesting.com
Printed in the USA
LVHW010557291019
635546LV00001B/143/P